THE STREET PARTY

Cara Browne

Cover by Penny Vere

Table of Contents

Chapter 1	5
Chapter 2	11
Chapter 3	14
Chapter 4	20
Chapter 5	25
Chapter 6	36
Chapter 7	40
Chapter 8	47
Chapter 9	53
Chapter 10	56
Chapter 11	71
Chapter 12	80
Chapter 13	84
Chapter 14	89
Chapter 15	97
Chapter 16	101
Chapter 17	112
Chapter 18	119
Chapter 19	122
Chapter 20	130

Chapter 21	132
Chapter 22	141
Chapter 23	148
Chapter 24	154
Chapter 25	163
Chapter 26	168
Chapter 27	184
Chapter 28	191
Chapter 29	198
Chapter 30	206
Chapter 31	211
Chapter 32	216
Chapter 33	219
Chapter 34	226
Chapter 35	233
Chapter 36	236
Chapter 37	242
Chapter 38	253
Chapter 39	263
Chapter 40	269
Chapter 41	271
Chapter 42	274

Chapter 43	278
Chapter 44	283
Chapter 45	285
Chapter 46	288
Chapter 47	292
Chapter 48	295

Chapter 1

The dew was cold under Mikey's bare feet as he pegged out the washing. The whitest whites and brightest coloureds were Joe's – a recent growth spurt had forced Mikey to kit him out anew from top to toe. He marvelled at how little difference there was in size now between his own things and the boy's, and felt a warm gladness at the transformation of the lad from terrified child to calm, self-possessed eighteen-year-old.

Wisps of barely discernible pink were beginning to streak the white-blueness of the sky, and as a bird sang out into the fresh, bright air and another trilled and chirruped in reply Mikey's heart stirred within him at the pitch of the different notes, the rhythm patterns, the magic of the mingling of the two. Then smiling his wide, wide smile and singing softly he shimmied back up the garden path.

. . . .

Shane sat in the lotus position in the middle of the living room floor, facing a huge poster of a full blown rose.

"Ro-ose," said Shane, slowly and distinctly, gazing at the picture. He took three long, evenly spaced breaths.

"Ro-ose," he repeated.

Behind him Susan was leaning out of the open window of their top floor flat, savouring the freshness of the air. Her fist was closed tightly around the two pound coins she had just stolen out of Shane's trousers, which had been thrown carelessly over the chair just inside the door of the bedroom he shared with Imogen, Susan's mother. Susan was always careful not to take enough to arouse suspicion.

"Mikey's always the first up in Cannon Street," she said. She had just seen him coming out of the side door of his house with a basket full of washing and disappearing into his back garden to hang it out. Being new to the street Susan was still trying to piece together who all the neighbours were.

"Ro-se," said Shane, "He isn't actually. Ro-ose".

"Who is then?"

Shane stood up. "Sid the milkman's the first up in this street," he said. "He has to be at the depot by three o'clock."

"Is he our milkman?"

"No. This street isn't part of his round. He just lives here. I'd better go and make your Mum's tea. Do you want some?"

"Yes please."

Susan continued to watch the street, particularly The Grange, the big house opposite, for signs of life. Apart from Mikey early morning sightings of the neighbours were rare, although once or twice she had seen each of the men who lived at The Grange coming home at first light. The one who drove the car seemed furtive when he came home at that time, closing the car door slowly and carefully so that it didn't make any noise. The posh one was quite the opposite, slamming the taxi door, then the front gate, knocking milk bottles over, cursing while he fumbled for his key. Sometimes he seemed to fall rather than walk through the front door, which he generally slammed loudly behind him. Susan was a light sleeper, and sometimes got out of bed and took a peek from behind her bedroom curtains to see what was going on.

Susan liked Shane, and now that Imogen's dependence had switched once more from her daughter to the man of the moment Susan's feeling was less of neglect, as it would have been four or five years ago, and more of freedom. Shane was likely to be around for some months, making it easier for Susan to come and go as she pleased for a while. However she knew she would have to be careful because she didn't want to be taken into care again.

. . . .

Puffing slightly Quentin, who was far from fit, got to the top of Park Street. Wedged between Millicent's Fabrics and The Koffee Kabin a tiny bookshop, tall, narrow and set back from the street, caught his eye. Why hadn't he noticed it before?   The building had obviously been there for decades, centuries even. A tingle of excitement ran through him. It was just the place where he might find some rare archaeological treatise which could help him with his research.

He pushed open the door, and the musical note which sounded led not into a little burst of tinkling and jingling as he expected but into the sound of jazz saxophone playing Little Brown Jug so infectiously that it brought the shadow of a smile to his face and made him want to tap his feet.

There was nobody in the room in which he found himself. A small counter piled with books stood to one side and the shelves, which reached to the ceiling, were filled to overflowing. There was a closed door in the wall opposite and the room, which had only one small window, was surprisingly sunny. He set about examining the contents of the shelves, dimly curious all the while about the jazz music in the background which continued to play.

Someone coughed and Quentin started. He turned and saw a slight, greasy-haired young man leaning over the counter, slowly turning the pages of one of the books on it. Quentin wondered a little uneasily how it was that he hadn't heard the man come in.

"Can I help you?" enquired the young man without looking up.

"Is there an archaeology section?"

The room had become dark and gloomy, and the fact that the sun had gone in so suddenly seemed ominous to Quentin. His euphoric mood evaporated.

"Archaeology, Ancient History and Gardening through the door, down the passage and fourth door on the left."

Quentin crossed to the door, opened it and entered an unlit passage. The door clicked shut behind him. He stood still in the darkness and felt for a light switch but could find none. It struck him that he could still hear the music, louder now – it had been fairly subdued in the shop.

His eyes gradually became accustomed to the darkness and he began to make his way slowly along the passage, feeling the wall on the left all the while so that he would be sure not to miss any of the doors and lose his way. The length and apparent direction of the passage surprised him. As far as he knew he was proceeding at right angles to the street from which he had entered the shop and was on the same level, but his knowledge of the area told him that if this was so he should have emerged into the next street by now. The music had become very loud indeed, and then he heard shouting ahead of him. He stopped and listened;

someone was calling. He recognised Kate's voice and strained to catch the words: "Hurry up Chloe! Quickly now!" Then the passage flooded with light, and the music was clearer than ever.

> *"Ha, ha, ha, hee, hee, hee,*
> *Little brown jug how I love thee ..."*

The words of the song skipped merrily through his head.

Quentin opened his eyes and saw the long, light curtains of his bedroom gently billowing, and from two doors down the street and through his open window came the joyful sound of Mikey's first saxophone practice of the day. He heard eleven year old Chloe's feet come clattering past his door and down the stairs, whilst in the drive below Kate's exasperated before-school voice turned to scolding Jack, Chloe's twin brother.

Quentin's gaze moved from the window to the top of the chest of drawers where the photograph of Simon on the Malvern Hills, hair blowing in the wind, smiled down at him. Groaning with the pain that suddenly swept over him, Quentin turned over and pulled the duvet over his head.

Chapter 2

The big house in which Kate, her husband David, the twins and, more recently, Quentin lived had a distinctiveness that set it apart from the rest of the street. The size and early Victorian grandeur of The Grange opened up endless creative possibilities for Kate's love of interior design, whilst its shabby condition and its location in a grubby street of unimaginative brick houses made it acceptable to David and his burgeoning ideologies.

A narrow path down one side of the garden, connecting the streets at the front and the back of the house, was so overgrown that it was hardly used – at least not as a path. From among its dusty foliage Susan was peering at Chloe and Jack, who were playing chess on the back terrace in the spring sunshine. The five occupants of The Grange, whose comings and goings were easy for her to observe from the windows of her home, were becoming a source of voyeuristic diversion to her, but it was the twins who interested her most, being close in age to herself and in the year below her at school. Now, as she looked on from her hiding place, she longed to join them. However even watching Chloe and Jack from a distance on this sunny Saturday morning was better than watching television alone in the stuffy flat, with the sound down so low so as not to waken her mother that she could barely hear it. Shane had already done his meditation and gone off to one of his gardening jobs.

Susan adjusted her squatting position, taking care not to catch on the surrounding brambles the expensive embroidered and sequined jeans Shane had bought her. Just then Kate came out onto the terrace carrying a tray laden with a jug of juice and a plate of little cakes and biscuits. Susan heard the sound of voices and fragments of conversation. Kate filled glasses from the jug whilst Jack and Chloe helped themselves from the plate. With a drink in her hand Kate strolled across the terrace and sat down at the top of the little flight of steps that led down to the unkempt lawn, and a moment later another figure, clad in a silk paisley dressing gown, emerged suddenly, as if catapulted, from the shadow of the French windows. It was Quentin. He spoke, though Susan couldn't make out the words, and Chloe jumped up and ran across and threw her arms around him.

Kate got up and came over to him and he put his arm lightly round her shoulders and kissed her on the cheek. Susan already realised that it was David, not Quentin, who was the father of the twins, but Quentin definitely seemed to be part of the family. Now it was Jack who got up from his seat and joined the others, and to Susan the four of them standing there looked so connected with each other that her throat tightened.

All at once she heard a sound like a dog coughing and Quentin was leaning over slightly. For a moment she wondered if he was about to vomit, then realised with a shock that he was crying.

Chapter 3

From his hiding place behind the Sunday Telegraph Quentin heard David come in and sit down at the kitchen table. The atmosphere changed as if at the flick of a switch. Taking the kettle from the Aga Kate made a pot of tea for David and a pot of coffee for herself and Quentin. Nobody spoke. Quentin, who was hung over and depressed on this particular day, never did at breakfast time whether the others did or not but simply read the paper, ate a piece of toast, drank some coffee and departed. He felt it prudent, for as long as he wished to stay with the Dawsons, to be discreet and not intrude in their marriage or family life in any way, and he deluded himself that he was achieving this by not turning their twosomes into threesomes more than could be helped. This suited Quentin anyway because he didn't like David and would not have sought out his company either with Kate or without her. Kate on her own was quite another matter.

Kate and Quentin had been neighbours when they were children. Quentin, an only child, had had archaeologist parents who were often away, leaving him in the care of a housekeeper if they were off on a trip while he was home from boarding school. However even when they were there they paid him little attention. Quentin became almost a brother to Kate, latching on in his loneliness to her and her father in their varied and absorbing activities, while Kate's careerist mother spent her time wandering around the

Cotswolds taking photographs for the country magazine she worked for. Having lost contact with one another over the years Quentin's and Kate's paths had unexpectedly crossed again through Simon, and this had rekindled their friendship.

Quentin drained his coffee cup for the third time and folded his newspaper.

"See you later," he said, and departed.

After weeks of arguing Kate and David still hadn't reached agreement about where to have the fast approaching Queen's Golden Jubilee Street Party – whether it was to be in Cannon Street itself or in their own large garden – and this was making them even more bad tempered with each other than usual. Neither could they agree about whether to have it on the actual day of the Queen's Golden Jubilee or the following weekend. Not, of course, that these were automatically their decisions by right, to make on behalf of the rest of the residents of Cannon Street, but they had been democratically elected to the post of Golden Jubilee Street Party Organisers by those who chose to be involved in this particular local celebration. People in general had been vague about what they wanted in terms of time and place, so it had been left to David and Kate to decide.

"Everyone is bound to want to watch the whole thing on telly," said Kate.

She'd mentioned this several times already, and tried not to let exasperation leak into her voice. "And it goes on all day. I really think it would be better to have the party on the Saturday."

David reached for another piece of toast and sighed.

"Everyone? I can't really see Joe and Mikey sitting on the settee all day long watching a load of overdressed toffs driving along in a golden coach. Or Mo and Myra. Or Amos and Dainty. And as you know," he added, "you can definitely count me out."

"Well, most of the older people will want to watch it – Kathleen for example – and so do I." Then primly, "And I think the children ought to watch it – it's a piece of history in the making and part of their heritage."

This last bit was a wind-up. David was not interested in history except as a tool for manipulating an argument, and he thoroughly disapproved of pageantry in any shape or form. He did not encourage his children to develop what he considered to be elitist sympathies.

"Well," he retorted, "it's only on the actual Tuesday that we could have it in the street – it's the only day that the road is officially closed. Your idea of having it in our garden sucks – it makes us look like the lord and lady of the manor. I might also remind you that they're called street parties because that's where people have them – in the bloody street."

"Not necessarily. It could simply mean that they're *for* the people who *live* in the street."

Before these words were even out of her mouth Kate felt annoyed with herself for surrendering the moral high ground by being so childishly argumentative, but she was finding it increasingly difficult not to rise to the bait. This particular battle was lost now, she knew, and the Cannon Street Golden Jubilee Party would almost certainly be held in the street on the first Tuesday in June. Maybe it would be possible to rig up a couple of tellies outside to keep everybody happy, thought Kate. The only way to preserve a shred of dignity now was to change the subject.

"Chloe has been invited to an open day at the Curzon Academy. I've said I'll go with her."

"The Curzon Academy? Is that sponsored by soap manufacturers?" It was some time now since David had been able to make Kate laugh with his feeble jokes.

"No. *Curzon*, not Cusson. It's a very prestigious dance school. She's been doing awfully well with her ballet recently, and it's a great honour that she's been noticed."

"There's no point in her enrolling in a professional dance school since she's not going to be a professional dancer."

Kate bristled. "I think that's up to her."

"Not while she's under my roof."

Kate believed (and Quentin agreed with her) that in spite of the insecurities of a dancer's life it was right to encourage Chloe to strive to fulfil her dream provided she was aware of the drawbacks. Deep down David agreed but wasn't going to admit it. Chloe herself did her part by working hard both at ballet and at ordinary school work. David's intransigence was largely caused by the fact that Kate often discussed things with Quentin before she discussed them with himself, and he felt that since Quentin had arrived among them he, David, had become hugely handicapped in the matrimonial negotiation stakes.

They sat there in silence, each pondering the next sally. At this point in the conversation neither of them was about to verbalise spontaneously – each had experienced many times the indignity of being out-manoeuvred by the other. David didn't want to make his gaff worse and Kate wanted to retain the moral advantage. Yet again each one was wondering whether there was any way they could save their relationship or whether they would end up separating.

The doorbell rang.

"I'll get it," said Kate, getting up. She went out through the hall and opened the front door, and by craning his neck David could just see Kathleen standing on the front doorstep.

Chapter 4

"More tea love?"

Wendy looked at her watch. "Yes, why not? Sid won't be awake for a while yet." She pushed her mug across to Kathleen.

"I see you've got one of those plastic tablecloths. Popular, aren't they?"

"It's not plastic, love. PVC. Stronger than plastic. Don't tear."

"Oh." Wendy looked dubious. PVC or plastic, it was all the same to her. She thought it looked a bit cheap and old-fashioned, all right for an old woman like Kathleen, but she herself preferred by far her own smart wipe-clean melamine-topped kitchen table with its wooden edging.

"They got one just like it in the kitchen up at the big house," said Kathleen airily. "Same colours an' all."

The big house was what many of the locals called The Grange.

"Been inside the big house then have you?"

"Day before yesterday. I was up there to see Kate about how many sausage rolls she wants me to do for the Jubilee Street Party."

"Kate? You mean Mrs Dawson?"

"She said to call her Kate."

"Oh. Did you see that bloke when you were up there?"

"What bloke?"

"You know. The posh one. With the suede shoes and silk scarves. Sometimes looks like Long John Silver."

She was speaking of Quentin who, conditioned no doubt by his years in one of those public schools whose uniform is somewhat archaic, sometimes showed off his shapely calves by wearing knee breeches, white stockings and buckled patent leather shoes together with a Regency style jacket. Now and then, when feeling particularly flamboyant, he added a three-cornered hat to his curly blonde hair. Apart from those infrequent occasions his normal daily dress, together with his elegant frame and easy style of walking, gave him a distinctly Noel Coward air.

"Oh, him. No, I didn't see him. He's been staying there a while now, hasn't he?"

"Over six months I should think. Funny to see someone like him walking around a place like this, isn't it? I mean, I know you mostly get quite a nice class of people round here these days, but decent and posh is two different things."

"It was posh enough round here in my gran's day, you better believe it. Really smart it was back then, with all the carriages going up and down to and from the big house. Busy too, what with all the scullery maids, chamber maids, cooks, valets and what have you going to and fro, before you even mentions the trades people making deliveries. Most of these other houses in Cannon Street have sprung up since then. It's nothing special at all now of course. But not scruffy any more like it was a few years back, thank goodness. Better folk have been moving back in lately – well, you know, like them up at the big house."

She noticed Wendy looking at her hard.

"And like you and Sid, of course," Kathleen added hastily.

Kathleen was very fond of Wendy in spite of her pretensions, and wouldn't hurt her feelings for anything. She knew that Wendy felt that she and Sid had moved up in the world. After all they were buying their own house, and Wendy had her sights set on opening her own hair salon once she had finished her apprenticeship at Mikey's Unisex Salon on Suffolk Place, just round the corner from Cannon Street.

Wendy would have liked her husband, Sid, to be more ambitious. He was intelligent and hard working so she could not understand why he seemed content to remain a milkman.

"Who sweeps a room as for His laws makes that and the action fine," Sid would say enigmatically whenever

Wendy urged him to better himself. Although she sometimes went to church with him the deeper levels of his faith were a mystery to her.

"It'll never be really posh down here again I don't suppose," said Wendy. "Pity."

"It's trendy now," said Kathleen. "I heard someone say so the other day. Trendy's more fashionable than posh."

"I suppose that's why it's a bit of a mixture round here. I can't say I'm happy about those two who've moved into number seventeen. The older one dresses like a tart if you ask me."

Wendy was a fairly ordinary-looking girl herself, decidedly on the plump side, whilst Imogen, to whom she was referring, had the kind of fragile, ethereal beauty that was attractive only to certain men but generally envied by other women. Kathleen wasn't sure whether it was prudery or jealousy talking.

"And they're not sisters like we thought, they're mother and daughter," Wendy continued. "Unfit mother if you ask me."

"You can't be sure of that, love, just because of the way she dresses. And the younger girl seems all right to me, except maybe she dresses too old. She looks sixteen, but I'll lay odds she's nearer twelve. Anyways you can't judge a book by its cover – look at Mikey and young Joe now – that lad's come on marvellous since Mikey's took him on. Everyone said that a single black hairdresser and worse still, night club musician, had no business trying to adopt a white boy with two parents of his own, but it looks like it was the best answer for everyone, 'specially Joe. Like I say, you can't always judge things from the outside, or whether someone's a good parent or not."

"True. Joe's really sorted now. He still comes into the salon sometimes but Mikey doesn't make him anymore, he can trust him to be on his own these days. Joe's changed a lot."

"I rest my case," said Kathleen. "I think I might call in on number seventeen later and make sure they know about the street party."

"Suit yourself," said Wendy.

Chapter 5

Quentin opened his eyes and looked at his surroundings – magnolia walls, ornate glass wall lights, Rococo mirror, lightly embossed cream curtains. He thought he recognised the room, but couldn't work out where it was. His tongue was dry and stiff, and the inside of his head was thudding. He eased himself up on his elbows and looked dejectedly but without surprise, having drunk continuously for almost two days, at the half-empty whisky bottle which stood on top of the television next to a glass with an inch of the amber liquid still in it. Next to these was the picture of Simon, which Quentin took with him wherever he went.

He tried to identify the loud, almost uniform noise that he could hear, until he suddenly realised it was the sound of heavy traffic. Gingerly he got up off the bed, and going to the window he was relieved to see the busy road and bustling pavements of Kensington High Street spread out below him.

Now he remembered that he was staying in his usual hotel in London for two different reasons. Firstly it was to go to Heal's again in an another attempt to find suitable settees and coffee tables for the house in the Oxfordshire countryside, the house with which he was still hoping to lure Simon back to himself. Secondly it was to talk to Ursula, one of the librarians at the British Library, about the paper he was writing, which was behind schedule. Inwardly this first aspect of the trip was making Quentin feel furtive if not downright guilty, as at different times both Kate and Ursula had gone to some lengths to persuade him to abandon the idea of a permanent relationship with Simon. It's for your own good, they had said, look at the evidence, Simon isn't interested. When in their company Quentin had paid lip service to this wise advice, and had been, on occasion, almost won over by it. But now nearly recovered from his second breakdown – Ursula had supported him through the first and Kate was still mothering him through the second – Quentin was realising that Simon had become an obsession, and that his pursuit of him was not a matter of choice. In a way he still imagined it to be love, but also recognised that it had become a compulsion against which he was powerless, and the continuing pursuit of Simon was the only thing that gave him relief from a constant sense of agitation. He felt unable to confess this to either Kate or Ursula. He feared that their support, which he might still need, could be withdrawn if he was not willing to do as they suggested. He therefore continued to succumb to the addiction whilst pretending that it had been renounced. Quentin's consolation at the end of every day was to indulge, during the moments before he fell asleep at night, in a fantasy of a future shared with his beloved.

Quentin's secret plan was to continue turning the Oxfordshire house into what he thought would be the perfect hideaway for a painter, in the hope that Simon would be unable to resist it, whilst pretending to Kate and Ursula that he was doing it only for himself. To the deluded part of Quentin's mind all this complicated manoeuvring felt quite normal, but occasionally the rational side of him woke up and watched with astonishment the lengthy unfolding of the whole saga, which had progressed from acquaintance to friendship, to the subliminal suggesting and rejecting of greater intimacy, and now to something distant and guarded. For the last three years contact had been minimal.

It was now about ten years since Quentin, then aged thirty-two and already a little jaded by life in the goldfish bowl of academia, first noticed the painfully reserved, radiantly beautiful eighteen-year-old Oxford University freshman and was instantly smitten, although the young man's behaviour was certainly strange. Simon was usually alone, and regularly seen going from place to place with the same even, purposeful walk. This gait never varied; no one saw him run or dawdle, and he always looked at the ground as he walked, as though wishing to avoid contact with other people. His natural reticence made him all the more alluring, and since he showed no interest in women, in fact if anything appeared to shun them, it was perhaps not particularly surprising that Quentin assumed that women did not attract him. Women admired him from a distance but few dared to approach. If they did he was neither friendly nor unfriendly, but he seemed uninterested in them and they didn't know what to make of him. Sometimes he spoke with male peers, who said he was a decent enough chap, but he was regarded as a bit odd. A few weeks after his arrival he joined the students' dramatic society and here, absorbed in drama and surrounded by the accoutrements of the theatre, Simon unexpectedly came out of his shell and started to behave like anyone else, but when theatricals were over for the day he became withdrawn once more. It was as though he was willing to engage with other people, but not as himself.

Quentin, as a lecturer, was not eligible to join the students' dramatic society but in an effort to strike up an acquaintance with Simon he hung around rehearsals, making himself useful by helping with props and suchlike. Eventually he built up a connection with him in a loose sort of way. Having discovered that he was reading history Quentin captured his interest by talking to him about the history of architecture and its place in archaeology. For several months Quentin focused on building a relationship with Simon based initially, and somewhat fraudulently on his own part, on theatre, though also to a lesser degree on history and archaeology, then gradually expanded the boundaries by engineering encounters at various events until Quentin felt it appropriate to invite Simon out for a drink after one of these.

A delightful two years ensued: plays, dinners, recitals, rambles, evenings with friends in country pubs, and occasionally a weekend away. From the start Simon seemed content to fall in with whatever Quentin suggested. It was tacitly understood that Quentin would always pay for everything – Simon could not have afforded any of these activities from his own finances. His quietness gradually changed to a chatty, friendly enthusiasm for the things they did. Such a lifestyle was completely new to him, and he was loving it.

During his own undergraduate years Quentin had pursued women in a desultory sort of way with little success. His lack of confidence and apparent lack of enthusiasm invited them to reject him. To him the species 'woman', in all its variations, felt alien. He was an only child and from the age of seven he had attended boys' only boarding schools, and as far as intimate personal relationships were concerned he had never progressed beyond the clandestine same sex passion of those early days. His distant and very beautiful mother was unfeminine in both daily dress and behaviour, doubtless due to the amount of time she spent clambering around archaeological sites and having to survive in a male-dominated world. Nevertheless on those occasions when formal wear was required she dazzled. She had an exquisite taste in clothes, and he and those around him watched, rapt, as she glided down the stairs on special occasions, looking for all the world like Audrey Hepburn in My Fair Lady. Then she was more goddess than mother, more apparition than woman. She was unique, and whether she was in dungarees or glad rags it never occurred to Quentin that fundamentally she was still simply a woman, albeit an extraordinary one, and he had never seen anyone so beautiful until he encountered Simon.

One day Quentin took Simon's hand as they walked through the mellow autumn countryside. It was immediately withdrawn. Quentin was disappointed, and unsure of whether to back off or make his interest more obvious. Over the months, almost imperceptibly, Simon became quieter, more remote, and although he continued to see Quentin something had changed.

Simon did not do well at Oxford. When he wasn't dallying with Quentin he had been dabbling with watercolours, indulging his secret passion of painting. Later it surprised even him, coming from the background he did, that he didn't take better advantage of the opportunity to gain a good degree from Oxford University, and with it a foothold on the ladder of worldly success. Instead, having been pushed through with a third, he had scuttled off to Dorset to become a painter.

Quentin had known at the time of his first emotional collapse (Kate had let it slip) that Simon's work wasn't selling well. He now suspected that it still wasn't, although Simon did have talent. It was partly to do with the fads of the time that influence buyers, but also Simon was rather inept at the business side of things. Furthermore it was likely that he hadn't yet fully matured as a painter, and thus the best of which he was capable had not yet manifested itself. Quentin knew, however, that life's finer things were very appealing to Simon, and that he liked to work with the very best materials, and so he could not conceive of Simon rejecting the opportunity to have the best of all possible worlds. He would convince Simon, once the Oxfordshire house was perfected in every detail, that the place needed to be lived in in order to maintain its sound condition until he, Quentin, decided to take up residence there himself at some unspecified time in the future. He would of course allow Simon to have the whole place rent free, bills paid, to himself for as long as it took. The time, money and effort that Quentin spent planning and, to a small degree, executing his plan to capture Simon made him able to bear not being with the man himself.

Ursula was a fellow archaeologist, and over the years she and Quentin had acquired considerable professional respect for each other. Familiarity had even caused Quentin to have a certain affection for her, though whether or not this was returned was questionable, for nobody had ever recorded seeing any sign of emotion at all in Ursula. Even her nursing of him through his first crisis had been a no-nonsense, practical affair. She was totally committed to her work – just as well some might have said, for an oil painting she was not, nor was she endowed in any obvious way with charm or that undefinable quality, sex appeal.

Quentin himself was highly involved with his subject but not in the same all-consuming way. Nowadays it played second fiddle to his obsession with Simon, and outside of that it was subject to his social and academic posturing. Because of her lack of distractions (as far as anyone knew Ursula had never had a hobby or a boyfriend) as well as her place of work it was Ursula who was up to date with everything, from what was happening on archaeological sites all over the world to the latest books and papers which had been written on the subject. From a work point of view Quentin's reliance on her was immense, and he needed more of her help now if he was ever to finish his own paper. One of the consequences of the difficulties in his personal life was that the violence of the resulting emotional roller coaster tended to eclipse other aspects of existence which were, accordingly, neglected. By consulting Ursula he could catch up quickly on most of the research which by rights he should have done himself.

In the few minutes since he had woken up in his hotel room Quentin's thirst had become unbearable, so he went to the bathroom and drank several glassfuls of water in quick succession then looked at himself in the mirror. He was surprised to find that he didn't look anything like as bad as he felt – in fact from his appearance you would have said that he seemed remarkably well. His watch told him that it was seven forty-five on Monday, which more or less fitted in with what his partially recovered memory told him. Because it was a twenty-four hour watch he knew it was around about breakfast time rather than supper time. There was plenty of time to get to his eleven o'clock appointment with Ursula at the British Library.

He wondered whether he should ring for room service and have breakfast brought up to him, but the thought of food made him heave. The sight of the glass and bottle on the television set was having much the same effect, so he took them into the bathroom and poured away all the whisky and dropped the empty bottle in the waste paper basket. He decided he would have a bath rather than a shower, which would give him a little time to mull over the events that last night had ultimately led him to consume a great deal more whisky in the space of a couple of hours than was his normal habit. He would then get himself down to the dining room and consume copious amounts of, firstly, orange juice for his terrible thirst and the vitamin C and, secondly, coffee, again for the liquid but also for the caffeine which might make him a bit more alert, but since it might make his headache even worse he rang down to room service for paracetamol, which could start taking effect while he was in the bath.

As Quentin swished the bubble bath round the bits of his anatomy which broke the surface of the water he realised that the anguish of Saturday morning, when once again the female voice had answered Simon's phone, had substantially subsided. Now forty-eight hours removed from that agony of emotion he found that he was able to think much more clearly and calmly. He set about providing himself with a set of reassuring facts to help him face the day and the rest of his life, or at least the next few days and weeks.

The first thing he reminded himself of was that nothing in particular had changed recently between himself and Simon, that presumably they were still friends, even though the friendship had been on hold for the last three years or so. And they had got on so well during the first couple of years they had had together. Surely this wouldn't have been the case if they hadn't really liked each other?

The second thing was that the fact that the same female voice had been answering the phone since he had secretly begun trying to contact Simon again did not necessarily mean that Simon had a girlfriend. Two days ago, the last time this had happened, Quentin had run out onto the terrace in a state of disbelief and fear, and then to his immense embarrassment had burst into tears in front of Kate and the twins. This had been difficult to explain away. He had muttered something about having had a terrible nightmare. But didn't he, Quentin himself, have women in his life on a very regular but totally non-intimate basis? Kate and Ursula for example – there was certainly no romance or intrigue between himself and either of them. But although Quentin himself had never been completely smitten by a woman (apart from his mother) he had never been sure about Simon's proclivities in this respect. Simon had always been brilliant at avoiding conversations he didn't want to have.

The third thing was that he, Quentin, had a sound strategy – that of offering his prey something that he had not the means to provide for himself – something that should greatly attract him – a fully equipped haven of matchless tranquillity where his imagination could run free and his talent blossom. Quentin himself would stay discreetly in the background until invited to approach, for surely Simon would eventually become his from pure gratitude. He, Quentin, would be the benefactor who had made all the Great Works, which under such conditions could not fail to be released from within Simon, possible. That was why, four and a half years ago, when it became clear that Simon was pulling away from him, Quentin had purchased the romantic but somewhat rundown house 'with potential' on the edge of a small Oxfordshire village.

Quentin climbed out of the bath and vigorously rubbed himself all over with the enormous fluffy towel. He then sat on the edge of the bed and slowly and carefully dried between his toes before sprinkling them liberally with talcum powder. Suspended in an alcohol-induced sense of unreality he dressed himself with habitual care, dried his hair using the diffuser head of his hairdryer and the little finger of his left hand to form the bubbly curls, then made his way towards the dining room.

Chapter 6

It was Friday night and the Dugout Jazz Club was heaving. People stood four or five deep at the bar or sat with their drinks around the small tables surrounding the dance floor. A few couples were dancing. The sweat was beginning to run into Mikey's eyes – in a minute he would have a chance to mop his brow – but for the moment he had settled into his playing and was able to look around at the same time to see which faces were familiar. There was one in particular he was looking for – heart-shaped and translucent with huge blue eyes and a mane of thick blonde hair surrounding it. He guessed she was around seventeen, and had first noticed her about six months ago. He sought her out with his eyes every Friday, which seemed to be the night she usually came, attracted not only by her looks but also by the group of friends she came with, who were lively and animated but never disorderly.

"She's here again then," said Amos, the clarinettist, during the next break. He had worked out for himself that Mikey would have liked her for Joe.

"Yeah."

"How you gonna get 'em introduced, then?"

"Huh?" asked Mikey innocently.

"Joe an' the li'l blonde? How you gonna get 'em together? They ain't gonna bump into each other on the

Gloucester Road now, are they? An' say 'hey, man, I was jus' lookin' for you, where you bin?' It ain't gonna happen unless you make it happen."

"Can't do that," said Mikey. "The kid's gotta live his own life."

"No harm in helpin', is there?"

"The fact is, I don't think he really wants a girlfriend."

"Don't wanna girl friend? Ev'body wanna girlfriend."

"Joe's cautious. Likes what he knows. Still doesn't trust folks too much. Know what I mean? He'll get there. Eventually."

"Havin' a girl gonna give him confidence, man. Be good for him."

"Gotta let him be the judge of that. You and me can't know what's good for another person. You might want it, I might want it, doesn't mean he's gotta want it. Live and let live, man."

Mikey would have loved to see Joe with a girlfriend. It would help reinforce and confirm his recovery from childhood trauma. But he wasn't concerned that it hadn't happened yet.

Joe, meanwhile, was playing snooker at Blues, his usual haunt on the Gloucester Road. His first exam was in a couple of weeks, but he understood the balance between work and play, and his scruffy mates were a nice bunch of lads. He had been at school with most of them, but unlike them he had been one of the very few not to leave at sixteen. This was a deal he had done with Mikey and now, hopeful of success in the impending exams, having studied hard for eighteen months, Joe was grateful that he had been pressed to stay on and do 'A' levels. Unlike the other kids he had a job with a local computer firm to go to at the end of June when his exams were finished. If he didn't get the hoped for results to get him into university, and didn't want to return to school for resits, he could stay on in the job.

Mikey was right in his belief that Joe didn't particularly want a girlfriend. It wasn't that Joe disliked girls, but at the time his peers had been beginning to experiment with the opposite sex Joe was struggling with the uncertainty of not knowing whether or not the child welfare people would allow him to go and live with Mikey officially, or whether he would have to stay with his natural parents or be taken permanently into care. He had stayed with Mikey on and off from the time he was scarcely more than a toddler during the times his parents were incapable of caring for him properly, or simply wanted relief from child care.   Joe's plight at the time had not reached the attention of the authorities, whom Mikey didn't particularly trust. Where Mikey came from people looked after their own, and Joe was his own, wasn't he? Wasn't it Mikey who had found him that first time twelve years ago, hiding behind the dustbins at the end of the alley, cold, wet, hungry and frightened? Wasn't it Mikey's door that Joe had learned to knock on every time he needed help? And when others had found him wandering the streets, wasn't it Mikey they took him to?

Joe desperately wanted to live with Mikey, but it had taken Mikey seven years, from the time when Joe himself was seven years old, to get the adoption through, and that had been against all the odds. All the expected objections had been thrown up – the racial difference, the fact that Mikey was a single male of an age where he could barely be Joe's biological father anyway and so on. Joe's parents made one or two half-hearted attempts to get him back, but since they seemed unable to modify their antisocial behaviour or reduce their drinking the threat was negligible. Mikey knew this, but it always frightened Joe, who was terrified of going back to his old life.

By the time Joe had settled into the patterns and standards of behaviour upon which Mikey insisted, and had begun to develop a sense of security, early adolescence had passed him by. This didn't bother him. He watched the mating rituals being performed around him by his peers, drew conclusions and decided that there was not much to be gained from the whole business except grief and complications, and decided that women could wait. If Mikey could have guessed that this was Joe's reason for not having a girlfriend he would have been impressed.

Chapter 7

Now that the disagreement over the precise time and place of the street party had been resolved preparations were under way and Kate was in her element. She hoped that there was sufficient time to do everything the way she wanted it done.

"Chill, man," Amos had said when he caught her rummaging feverishly among the spice jars in the Caribbean supermarket on Suffolk place, searching for the ingredients Mo needed to make the special curry he had promised to contribute to the occasion, providing she did the shopping for it.

"Heavens, Amos. Sometimes I wonder if I'm going to be ready in time for this wretched street party."

"What's to get ready? Jus' a few bit o' food to be trown together an' Bob's your uncle."

"You men haven't got a clue," snapped Kate, irritated by his insouciance.

People were in and out of The Grange every day on street party business. Some – probably those with most time to fill (Kathleen was one) – were making a major drama of it, popping in almost hourly on one pretext or another. Kate was thoroughly enjoying this. She had hardly ever managed to find time to invite people in for coffee, what with her ongoing renovations to the house as well as the daily round of a mother and housewife. Now she had the chance to spend a lot of her time in the kitchen, which suddenly seemed to have become a local community centre, since of course the main item on the party agenda was food and drink, and this involved a lot of chat and gossip with her helpers.

"Come on, Dainty, let's start ticking off the food list. Brew up another jug of coffee could you, Piety, there's a dear."

Dainty was Amos's wife and Piety, her unmarried sister, lived with the couple. Between the three of them they ran The Sceptre pub. The girls' mother, so family folklore had it, had named each of her infants within five minutes of its birth according to the characteristics she had wished for it at the time. As it turned out Dainty was a hefty lass, so far childless, whereas Piety was pregnant, though by whom she wasn't saying.

"Don't see no roti on this here food list," said Dainty.

"Roti?" said Kate.

"You wrote down chicken and rice?" asked Piety, putting a filter paper into the coffee machine.

"Jacaranda's bringing that," said Kate.

"I'll make the roti," said Dainty. "Amos won't come if there ain't no roti. You telling me, Kate, you ain't never et roti?"

"I'll fry up the yams and plantains on the day at the last minute," said Piety, "and bring 'em down hot."

Someone knocked and the kitchen door opened. It was Kathleen.

"I've only popped in for a moment dear, just to tell you I've been talking to them at number seventeen."

"Oh, yes, Imogen and Shane."

"Oh ... I didn't realise you knew them."

"I don't really, but the children know who they are, you know what kids are like, they're at school with the daughter. I've never actually spoken to any of them."

"Well, she says she'd like to help – she's a bit shy I think, but her bloke persuaded her. She wondered if you'd like her to make some trifle or something, but nothing foreign she says, I think she means ethnic love, she doesn't know the recipes. She doesn't like to come on her own, so I said I'd bring her round sometime if that's all right with you?"

"Of course. I'll look forward to seeing you both."

"Coffee's ready," said Piety, as Kathleen disappeared again.

Kate couldn't remember feeling so happy for years. For once she didn't feel it necessary to conceal from David her enthusiasm for food preparation, colour schemes and flower arrangement, because the whole project was going ahead with his approval. One of David's redeeming features was his sense of community, and his displeasure with her for preferring to be home-based rather than out being active in the field of social work appeared to be temporarily suspended. He had been less hostile these last few days, and Kate wondered if it was because he had triumphed over the location of the street party, although things had been so strained between them for the last couple of years that she wondered whether something so essentially trivial could really have altered his mood that much, or whether there was some completely different reason. She would have liked to think that he was coming to terms with the fact that she wasn't the person they both believed her to be when they married, but she thought it unlikely.

Kate's father had died when she was nine. The shattering of the charmed life she had led with this gentle, intelligent, companionable man left her bereft. The youthful Quentin loyally continued to put in an appearance at regular intervals, but things just weren't the same. After the funeral and her rapid remarriage, and maybe because of her retreating youth, Kate's mother abandoned any pretence of running the home and started to devote all her time to her career and socialising with her new, mega-wealthy husband. A resident housekeeper was employed, and from the time Mrs Davis moved in with Emma, her fatherless daughter, Kate began spending a significant part of her time in the kitchen with the two of them. There she always found a welcome, with simple friendship and affection, quite unlike the rigid etiquette and unfriendly atmosphere of the rest of the house. Kate had never been close to her mother and she thoroughly disliked Keith, her stepfather. Neither did she have any time for his two snobbish children, Daphne and Elliott. When any of these four had the time or interest to notice what Kate was doing – which was rare – she was discouraged from mixing with 'the domestic staff'. Their obvious belief that Mrs Davis and Emma were distinctly inferior beings ignited a resentment in Kate that grew as time passed. It was the intensely felt ideas about justice and values that came into being during this phase of Kate's life that led her to the university course in sociology where she met David.

When David first married Kate everything had been very clear. David's father's perennial anger about social injustice had rubbed off on David. And Kate, in spite of the classy background that was part of her attraction for David, had unequivocally endorsed his views when they first met. If this hadn't been the case he could never have married her. But something had changed.

Kate had reverted to type.

When they first met, in their youthful naiveté they agreed passionately about things like equality of opportunity, protection for the weak and vulnerable, the creating of a fair society. They married within the year on a cloud of youthful euphoria. She had thought that they would go out into the world together and make it a better place. She still believed in the importance of that. But she had found David's militancy increasingly intimidating. She wanted to change the world and achieve justice by education and kindness and understanding. David seemed to want to do it through confrontation. When they obtained their degrees in sociology and their first jobs David was raring to go, to get out into the world and set it to rights, and rapidly and enthusiastically engaged in a round of committees, reports and legislation. Kate, on the other hand, soon found that she wasn't really enjoying the world of social work but was afraid to say so. She hated the reports and committees – she found them boring and not always helpful. She was alarmed at the hostility and lack of co-operation from many of those she was trying to help. She was perplexed by the fact that she didn't like many of her colleagues, let alone agree with them, and that many of them didn't seem to like her.

Kate began to have bouts of nostalgic reminiscing about the childhood years she had spent with her beloved father. Then when she discovered she was pregnant with the twins she told David quite truthfully that she had no idea why ten, consecutively, of last month's contraceptive pills were still in their blisters, but was intensely relieved to be able to stop work, at least for a time. She fell into a contented anticipation of life as a mother with the power to create for her children a carbon copy of the elegant, gentle life which she and her father had been unable to conclude. But she did not speak of this to David. It was only later that he gradually began to realise that Kate had no intention at all of going back to social work if she could avoid it. In the meantime invisible barriers, which they both sensed but never spoke of, began to grow up between them. Kate was always grateful, however, for any respite in their ongoing discomfort with each other and now, on the occasion of the Queen's Golden Jubilee, for the time being at least she did not need to be furtive or feel guilty about doing the things she enjoyed. And for once David had no sarcastic remarks to make about people spending time in this way since it was part of getting the job done.

Chapter 8

It was Sunday morning and the sun was streaming in through the French windows. David was sitting in his favourite armchair, apparently reading the paper but actually lost in his own thoughts. Earlier, before it got too hot, he had been digging in the vegetable patch – the only well-organised part of the garden. It was something he enjoyed doing, as his father had before him. When David was a child growing the vegetables had been a man's job.

Jack was trying, unsuccessfully, to play a tune on the piano.

"Where were you on Friday night, Dad?"

"I have meetings on Friday nights. You know that."

"Yes, but after the meeting."

"After the meeting I came home, of course." Something prompted him to add, "I had to drop Harry off first."

"Did you go in and have coffee with him?"

"Yes. Why?" David's face suddenly felt very hot, and he hoped he wasn't blushing noticeably.

"I just wondered. You got home so late. I heard the car at two o'clock in the morning."

"We had a lot to talk about."

David was rattled. He was used to coming and going as he pleased, without his whereabouts being questioned. Kate was accustomed to the fact that he worked irregular hours, as it was sometimes necessary for him to make house calls in the evenings and at weekends, and although he wasn't conscious of the fact she quite liked it if he wasn't at home too much. She never asked him where he'd been or why he was late, and he didn't now want his kids starting to monitor him. Not that he had ever had anything to hide – not until now at least, and even now he wasn't doing anything all that reprehensible – not so far anyway.

Normally at this time on a Sunday morning the twins would be out in the garden, engrossed in one of their complicated games, but this morning Kate had taken Chloe to an unscheduled dancing practice on account of an exam that was looming. Jack was lonely and bored, being much more dependent on his sister's company than she was on his. He had found things increasingly difficult over the last couple of years since ballet had taken over her life. He had begun, fearfully, to absorb the reality that he and Chloe were not going to be together in the same way for ever, that they would grow up, get jobs, even marry. It scared him a lot.

Kate had gone to some lengths to get Jack involved in some interesting activity of his own, but he had trouble in sticking to anything for long. He watched television happily enough while Chloe was at her after school dance classes, and during her normal weekend lesson on Saturday morning he usually went to the recreation ground with a group of friends to play football, so say, although most of the time was spent playing on mobile phones, scrapping and generally messing about, and sometimes no football was played at all. Now, half standing, half sitting on the piano stool he idly tried to pick out one of the simple tunes he had learnt during his brief flirtation with piano lessons. He kept playing the same phrase over and over again until David finally exploded:

"For heaven's sake, Jack, haven't you got anything to do?"

"No," said Jack sulkily. "I'm waiting for Chloe to come back."

"Well, she won't be back for some time. Go and find something to do. I'm trying to read the paper."

Jack slouched out of the room and directed his steps towards the kitchen. There was a chance that Quentin might be there having breakfast. Jack and Chloe found Quentin good company at any time of day. He could be a bit remote at times but was never irritable with them. They actually liked being with him better than they liked being with David. Quentin was larger than life. He always seemed pleased to see them and willing to talk to them. They loved the fact that from time to time he wore fancy dress – breeches with stockings and buckled shoes together with a Regency coat that he had specially made, and a three-cornered hat. He sometimes even went to work in this garb. David's conversation was usually about what people ought or ought not to do, about things his work colleagues did that annoyed and frustrated him, about things his clients did that couldn't be allowed. People he knew who came to the house were few, and seemed serious and dull. Quentin was warm, interesting, unpredictable and funny. At times he could be moody, withdrawn or neurotic but no one ever took it personally. He had all kinds of stories to tell – things that had happened when he had been an undergraduate, things that happened on various archaeological digs that he had been on or knew about, and a multitude of other things besides. Sometimes when he went away he brought them back something of archaeological interest, of value even, though he had to be careful about this. These were not gifts that the average eleven year old would receive, and they might be accompanied by a spellbinding yarn. He never talked down to them. Even David didn't object to the twins spending time with Quentin, although jealousy might have got the better of him if he had been a more assiduous father. David's jealousy confined itself to Quentin's relationship with Kate.

The kitchen, however, was empty when Jack got there and Quentin was nowhere to be seen. Jack felt quite spooked by the quietness. The bright sunshine showed up specks of dust moving slowly in the air, something that always made him wonder if it was safe to carry on breathing.

The ticking of the kitchen clock and the slow drip of the tap seemed very loud, as did Jack's own footsteps as he walked across the flag-stone floor to the back door, which led onto the terrace.

Once outside Jack began to feel better. The silence was gone. The light, warm breeze caused a faint rustling among the fresh young foliage on those trees whose leaves were already out. He heard the voices of passers-by from the street at the bottom of the garden and a motorbike speeding past on the road at the front of the house. He suddenly thought of going to see the rabbits, his and Chloe's, and was startled to realise that he could have done that to start with, that he didn't have to wait for Chloe to be here before he could do anything. This was a great revelation – there is life outside life with Chloe. He ran to the cage and rattled his finger down the wire. This brought Flopsy and Cottontail lolloping up to the wire where they nibbled at Jack's fingers.

"Want some dandelions, guys?"

He turned and went to look for some. He wandered over to the fence next to the path, because the biggest and juiciest dandelions were to be found round the edges of the garden. As he approached there was a sudden violent commotion among the bushes on the other side of the fence. Jack stood and stared. He couldn't imagine what on earth it was. It stopped. He waited for a moment then, more cautiously this time, with his eyes on the bushes rather than scouring the margins for dandelions he moved slowly forward, and the rustling and shaking began again. Finally he perceived something among the foliage. It was that girl from across the road. She stood up and, rooted to the spot with surprise, he watched as she pulled apart the unbuttoned front of her blouse to reveal tiny nipples atop two barely perceptible swellings. They stood looking at each other for what seemed an age, then Jack turned and ran full tilt back into the house.

Chapter 9

Now that Sid had finished washing and dressing he was properly awake. There was hardly any moon, but there was just enough light from a distant street lamp for him to locate Wendy's sleeping face. He kissed her softly on the cheek and tiptoed out.

It was getting towards the time of year that Sid loved best. He shut the garden gate and looked up at the sky. The slender new moon was still bright, but by the time he set out from the depot the blackness of the sky would have lost its depth and when he made his first drop at around five o'clock the sky would be pale grey, and at six o'clock he would be able to make an educated guess as to what kind of morning it was going to be – dull or bright, wet or dry. His pleasure in his job was heightened during these lighter mornings of spring and early summer.

The far-from-new car started first time as usual, in spite of Wendy's dark warnings that it would let them down any day now if they didn't do the sensible thing and purchase a new one with the aid of a loan such as were generally available these days, even to such ordinary folk as themselves.

Occasionally Sid got to work without having seen a single soul on the way, but not often. Even during the quietest times of the week it was usual to pass a pimp or a couple of local ne'er-do-wells on their way to or from a bit of drug dealing, but since a quarter to three on a Saturday morning, which it was, was still Friday night to some, the street had a fair sprinkling of revellers on their way home. However the first person he saw was Mikey – earlier than usual this morning – he was already turning into Cannon Street as Sid was turning out of it. Mikey was always pretty tired when he came home from the club and his step lacked its usual bounce in the small hours when he and Sid passed each other, the one on his way to work, the other on his way home. Sid wound down his window and they went through their usual ritual:

"You look tired, son. Drinka pinta milk a day. How many times do I have to tell you?"

Mikey laughed. His teeth looked even whiter at night. "Gecha hair cut. Come in this afternoon and I'll give you a perm half price. Highlights trown in for free."

To the casual observer Sid and Mikey weren't really that well acquainted, but deep in the heart of them they knew each other well. Mikey, with his upbeat personality, relaxed and extrovert and happy with the world, had a deep connection with the apparently unremarkable little man who delivered milk. Their interests were quite different. Sid wasn't interested in jazz and Mikey wasn't interested in growing vegetables and carnations. Mikey thrived on stimulation and new ideas, Sid preferred routine and predictability. Yet each had a capacity for empathy that bordered on telepathy. Each was totally trusted by the community in which they lived, as well as being slightly detached from it. Most importantly, each knew how to keep his own counsel – Mikey often played father confessor to the occupants of the barber's chair, and the goings-on that Sid was party to, simply by being up and doing at a time when most folk were still in bed, did not bear thinking about. They each observed a self-imposed code of confidentiality. See no evil, hear no evil, speak no evil. Each was entirely his own man.

As Sid proceeded along Balmoral Road he noticed the Dawson's beige space wagon parked by the side of the road about half way down, which wasn't really surprising because he had been on the lookout for it. Keeping his gaze straight ahead so as not to pry he could nevertheless see inside the car with the tail of his eye as he drove past. It wasn't the first time that David had been parked there, sitting in the driver's seat with his arm round a woman of indeterminate appearance. See no evil. Sid reached forward and pressed a switch. His Songs of Fellowship tape began to play and he started to sing along with it:

> *Bind us together, Lord bind us together*
> *With cords that cannot be bro-o-ken.*
> *Bind us together, Lord, bind us together,*
> *Bind us together with love.*

Chapter 10

Simon came down the stairs to see a hand-addressed letter in a pale lilac envelope lying on the doormat next to a couple of routine brown ones. Not many people wrote to him other than on official business – it was mostly e-mails and text messages these days. Curious, he picked it up and immediately recognised Kate's handwriting. Of course. By temperament rather than by age Kate qualified for the generation that regarded hand written letters as a normal, or even *the* normal, way of communicating with friends and family at distance. After leaving Dorset she used to write to Simon occasionally, as he now remembered, but he hadn't heard from her at all for some time, in fact he had temporarily forgotten about her existence. He had been preoccupied with family issues as well as his painting. The rebuilding of his relationship with his sister, Sheila, was foremost in his mind. He had recently had a brief meeting with her, the first for ten years, and a second, longer one was about to take place.

Dear Simon,

It's a long time, I know, since I last wrote, but both Quentin's presence here (which you may know about) and the events before his arrival have been an inhibiting factor in this respect. All the same, you haven't written to me either, you villain, whether for the same reason or because of your inherent indolence I shall refrain from asking. Or perhaps your life at the moment is so all-absorbing that you are not much interested in things outside it. If this is the case I insist that you tell me what's going on!

I've got a good excuse, which is to say a real reason, for writing at the moment, which stops me worrying that Quentin will think that my intention is to moan about him or to relay subversive information about him – you know how paranoid he is (he knows too of course).

This is a formal invitation to our street party on 4th *June in honour of Her Majesty's Golden Jubilee. I think it is only fair to Quentin to say that to invite you was my idea, mainly because the twins and I would love to see you. So would Quentin of course, but he's a bit hesitant about getting in touch again on a one to one basis after your year of total withdrawal – from him at least – to get on with your work (how is it going?) And while I'm at it perhaps I should point out on his behalf that this so called year of total withdrawal has turned into three!*

I think it could be time for the pair of you to break the ice again (is that the right expression?) if you'd like to come. You can see him as well as us on a kind of low key, casual basis. We have done some Serious Talking, Quentin and I, and he has concluded (so he says) that it would be lovely to see you sometimes if you feel the same. And honestly, Simon, the pair of you really did get on together so well, though of course it's none of my business. Quentin has confessed to being obsessive and suffocating in the past where you were concerned, but greatly values the time the two of you spent together and he says that he would welcome the opportunity to continue his friendship with you on a less claustrophobic (for you) basis. He insists that it would be no more intense than you wanted it to be. Anyway, if you come to see us you can make up your own mind.

David and I are not getting on any better – in fact things are far worse between us. He thinks I should have a job, and it's true that one income really isn't enough for us to manage on, what with all the refurbishments he has graciously consented to me undertaking, but I really don't want to go back to social work. I was young when I made that decision and it was a mistake. I would like to work again soon, but the twins still need a lot of supervision, especially living in an area like this, infested as it is with crime and drugs and other social problems.

I've decided to retrain – I want to do a course in interior design, which David doesn't approve of because he doesn't want his wife doing something so elitist, he says. Elitist?! When I point out that décor is an environmental issue which can impact significantly on social behaviour, he goes quiet and ends the conversation. I'm afraid that we may end up separating, and on a bad day that's what I think I want. It's very depressing.

Do you remember me talking about Keith, my grotesque stepfather and his gruesome children, Daphne and Elliott? Well, would you believe it, I've just had a letter from Daphne asking if we would mind having her daughter, Natasha, to stay for a few days. She says that Natasha is thinking of making Bristol University her fall-back position should she not obtain the Oxford place that everyone expects of her. Apparently Natasha wants to come and get the feel of the city of Bristol itself before she decides – Oxford of course she already knows inside out, both her parents were there and her brother Raj is there now. I've asked David, since I feel obliged to say yes, as we are obviously well placed to point Natasha's explorations in helpful directions, and

59

surprisingly he agrees, although he's unlikely to see much of her anyway. I think he's in for a bit of a shock if she turns out to be anything like Daphne!

The twins are growing up, Chloe a bit too fast, Jack not fast enough. She's well on the way to building a life of her own and he doesn't like it. He's getting left out and left behind but can't seem to sort out a direction for himself. I should welcome any suggestions/comments you wish to make, should you deign to accept this invitation. Far be it from me to put you under any pressure – but please come!

Lots of love, Kate

Simon stroked his chin. Then he read the letter again to discover exactly where it was that he had smelt a rat, sensed an incongruity. He stopped at "***he's a bit hesitant about getting in touch again ... and this so called year has turned into three.***" That's it, he thought. The old rogue. She thinks that he hasn't been in touch since I asked him to leave me alone for a year at least. But those unidentified phone calls that Sheila took recently, while I was painting ...I'm sure that was him, who else would it have been? In which case he obviously hasn't been telling Kate the whole truth. I think he's been trying to get in touch, even if he hasn't succeeded. And what about that call he made a couple of years back, telling me that *he* was too busy to see *me*? What was that all about? Presumably Kate doesn't know about that one either. All things considered it seemed reasonable to assume that Quentin hadn't told Kate the truth about a lot of things, which made it difficult to choose whether or not to accept this intriguing invitation.

Simon was actually very fond of Quentin, but he had become tiresome in certain ways, and after three years of painting in Dorset it had eventually seemed preferable to Simon, in spite of theatre visits, consignments of painting materials and meals in expensive restaurants, all regularly paid for by Quentin, to ditch him as gently as possible.

Kate herself hadn't spoken to Simon at all since that time three years ago, when she had phoned him to say that Quentin seemed to be having some sort of breakdown and that she thought that Simon, as a long-term friend of his, ought to know. Simon had replied that he was sorry that he couldn't help in any way, but pressure of work prevented it. He told her that he had recently informed Quentin of this same pressure of work and asked him not to get in touch for a year or so. Kate hadn't needed to be a rocket scientist to work out that it was this request from Simon that had probably caused the first breakdown. She had gratefully left the problem of Quentin in Ursula's capable hands and, torn by divided loyalties, she had withdrawn for the time being from Simon.

Ursula's success in rehabilitating Quentin had turned out to be short-lived, though Quentin himself was the only one who knew how short-lived. Two years ago, after a year of dedicated effort on Ursula's part he had had his first relapse after making, in a fit of misplaced confidence, what he had intended to be his last ever phone call to Simon, who gave him the cold shoulder and brought him crashing down again.

Now, however, cocooned at this present time by family life with the Dawson's and recovered from recent excesses (at least until his most recent stay in Kensington High Street), Quentin was doing it again. He had allowed himself to be taken over, for the *second* time, by the same phoney confidence, the recurring belief that he could now deal with the risk of rejection and that it was worth another try. Such was the nature of his addiction. In fact he had only phoned Simon occasionally, and only over the last two or three months. For better or worse Quentin had failed to establish contact until the last two attempts, when the same female voice had answered the call and Quentin had immediately hung up. He was now in serious danger of another relapse, especially as in his ambivalence he had failed to discourage the oblivious Kate from inviting Simon to the street party.

Kate and Simon had met quite independently of Quentin. It had been on a hot June day seven years previously. Kate had been on the homemade cake and jam

62

stall at a fete in a field in the Dorset countryside, where she and David had lived since just after the twins were born. The twins, at that time almost five years old, had been left to play at a friend's house on that particular day. Kate was delving in the basket at her feet in search of further supplies to replace on the trestle table those which had already been sold.

"Got any flapjack?" a voice said to her bottom, which was the only bit of her visible from the other side of the table.

She stood up, her face flushed from bending over, and was astonished at the loveliness of the face smiling at her. She responded with her own quirky smile.

"Half a tic," she said, and bent over again, and surfaced a minute later triumphantly clutching the required merchandise.

She wrapped the flapjacks and he paid for them, smiling at her all the while. She had no way of guessing at the delight inside him at finding himself in such a charming environment that he forgot that women under fifty alarmed him. Wanting to be friendly she said,

"Are you on holiday? I don't remember seeing you before."

The village in which they lived was small, and she knew most of the people at the fete. The young man had an astonishing presence, though whether or not this was simply because of his looks she couldn't tell.

"I moved in last week." She heard a pleasing mixture of BBC English and Cockney twang.

"Oh, really? Then welcome, neighbour."

She felt absurdly pleased at this information, but it was always exciting when someone new came to the village, and he was only the fourth new arrival since they had come themselves. So she said,

"You must come to dinner next week." Thus their friendship had begun.

It was in fact the following day that Simon made his first call to the Dawson residence. He went to borrow a tea towel and some string. The village shop, though open for limited hours on Sundays, did not stock these items, and the town was a five-mile bus ride away and in any case the shops would have been closed. There was no bell or knocker so he rapped on the door with his knuckles.

"Come in!"

David was sitting in an armchair that had seen better days, watching a sports programme on television. Kate and the twins were sitting round the large scrubbed kitchen-cum-dining table playing a board game. Simon's mind lurched and catapulted back over a decade or so to when he and his sister, inseparable companions that they were, had played board games almost daily. A picture of Sheila's twelve-year-old face flashed across his mind's eye.

"Take a seat, Simon, I'll put the kettle on. David, say hello to Simon. He's come to live in the village."

"Hello Simon," said David without looking up.

"Are you going to live with us?" enquired Jack.

"No. I've found myself a cottage to live in. It's near here, though."

"A tumbledown cottage?"

"Well, actually, the roof does leak a bit but it's not too bad. It's only in one corner."

"How are you settling in?" asked Kate, reaching up for mugs. "Tea or coffee?"

"Tea, please, white with one. It's gone pretty well on the whole. I haven't got much stuff anyway. I've only just finished my degree, and it doesn't take too long to relocate the contents of a student flat!"

"Where did you do your degree?" asked Kate. "And what in?"

"Oxford, and history."

"The first toff of the village," said David.

There was a pause. Then,

"My father is a carpenter actually," said Simon.

There was another brief silence.

"Would you like to try one of these cakes?" said Kate quickly. "Chloe helped me make them, they're delicious." She hoped David wasn't going to be sufficiently objectionable to stop Simon dropping in again.

"What brings you to this part of the world?" asked David.

"I want to start painting. Pictures, that is. This seems a peaceful enough place."

"Sounds great," said Kate quickly, before David got a chance to make a tacky comment. "What kind of thing?"

"Probably watercolours at first, rural topics and scenes, that kind of thing. It's a fairly common way to begin. I started dabbling when I was still at Oxford."

Kate was wondering what he was going to do for money, but didn't like to ask. Perhaps he's got a private income, she thought, or maybe he's had a windfall.

"I'll have to get a job," Simon had said. "Something simple that leaves my mind fairly free. It doesn't have to be well-paid but would preferably be part-time – a bar job perhaps, or working on the land."

"As long as you could manage on that."

Simon had not thought it apposite to mention his philanthropic friend at this juncture, although it was Quentin, hoping as he was to hold on to Simon, who had paid six months' rent in advance on the cottage. It was a year after this that Quentin had bought the house in need of renovation in a delightful corner of Oxfordshire.

"All part of the minimalist pose," said David from the depths of his armchair.

Why is this nice lady with this arsehole, wondered Simon.

"They'll be awarding a very poor degree," he said, "so it's no use looking for a posh job."

"Aren't you very bright, then?" joked David.

"I was considered a reasonable historian at one time," said Simon, "but I didn't do much work at Oxford, which made the exams rather hard to do."

Half an hour later Simon had departed with a dinner invitation for the following Saturday evening, leaving Kate and the children quite animated and David somewhat surly.

"Queer as a coot," said David.

"I don't think so," said Kate. David always claimed that he could detect such things, but she thought she knew better.

"What's a coot?" asked Jack.

"It's a bird," said Chloe.

Kate was in no doubt that Simon, like Quentin, was someone that David was not going to take to.

After that first dinner date Kate and Simon had met mostly during the week, when David was at work. David had been quite happy about this. He didn't see Simon as a threat and had no wish himself to spend time in his company. To Kate, being with Simon was very like being with her old friend Quentin but easier, for Simon had all of Quentin's charm and intelligence, though in a less flamboyant way, and none of his obtuse moodiness and self-absorption.

However Simon did have prolonged quiet moods.

"What are you thinking about?" Kate had asked him on a couple of these occasions, but he changed the subject without answering. She eventually noticed that in general he seemed reluctant to talk about his family. When she mentioned this to David he said,

"So what? It's often like that with families, for heaven's sake. Look at your own."

The first time Quentin had come to stay with Simon for a few days the joyful reunion between Quentin and Kate, which neither had anticipated, had Simon almost fishing for his hanky. Their previous meeting had been the one where, prior to her marriage to David, Kate had summoned her old friend, whom she hadn't seen for many years, in order to introduce him and David, her new fiancé, to each other – an encounter so unsuccessful that until now it had remained Quentin's last meeting with either David or Kate. The antipathy between the two men at that introduction had been so instant and complete that the patchy correspondence that had taken place between Quentin and Kate since he had left home to become an Oxford undergraduate came to an end. Quentin was hoping at this time of rediscovering Kate in Dorset that his relationship with Simon had simply encountered something of a hiccup, and said nothing about its true nature to her. Nevertheless after this meeting their correspondence resumed. He rarely wrote to Simon however, as writing wasn't immediate enough to meet his emotional need. Quentin always communicated with Simon by telephone.

The following year David, feeling that his professional capacities were sadly under-stretched, had left his job and started a new one in Bristol. At first he commuted weekly as Kate was reluctant to deprive the twins of their bucolic existence, but David found the travelling more and more difficult, so six months later Kate and the children moved to

Bristol too. Then Kate, having re-established a correspondence with Quentin, now began one with Simon. It was the correspondence with Quentin that survived and that with Simon that lapsed when she sensed that the role of intermediary was about to be thrust upon her at the time of Quentin's first breakdown.

Chapter 11

Tracy was examining her face in the mirror of the ladies' cloakroom, first right profile, then full face, then left profile. She licked her finger and passed it carefully over each eyebrow in turn, then teased a few wisps of hair forward over her face. The door from the passage opened.

"Very sexy," drawled Tulip. Tracy didn't like the way she said it, but from the lack of expression on Tulip's ebony face, now next to her own in the mirror, she could detect no malice.

"You going to the Cannon Street party?" David had pinned up a general invitation to anyone in the department who cared to come.

"Maybe. Our street isn't having one."

"Ours neither."

"Better hurry, we'll be late."

The two women hurried out and scuttled down the corridor to the conference room.

The others, ten in all, were already there, David behind the desk in front of the whiteboard and the remainder sitting on the wooden chairs which had as usual been arranged in a semi-circle facing him. Some were leafing through papers while others chatted or simply waited in silence. Each always sat in the same place as surely as if his or her name had been written on the seat, and Tracy took her accustomed perch on a chair at the centre of the semi-circle. She placed her bag on the floor and took a folder from it. She crossed her legs and carefully arranged her skirt so that the hem just brushed the top of her knees. She felt for the wisps of hair around her face and gave them another gentle tweak. David, flattered by his belief that all this was for his benefit, saw her do it without looking directly at her.

He looked up with a smile. "Are we all here? Good. The minutes of the last meeting then."

Someone cleared their throat and there was a slight shuffling of papers and feet. No one spoke. David sighed. I'd like to put a bomb under this lot, he thought. What he perceived as their general apathy over the last several months was affecting his own motivation. He wanted a team who reflected the reforming zeal with which he had entered the social services, and from time to time over the years he had worked with such groups and individuals, but this lot was so dull and uninspired. Some were, in his opinion, too old. Others were transparently bigoted. Some were young, and their energies, enthusiasm and commitment should be at their highest. The three over-forties among the group in front of him were stubbornly opinionated. It didn't occur to him that any of the problems related to his running of the department.

No issues were raised over the minutes of the previous meeting.

"OK. Let's get on with the rest of the agenda." He looked across at Tulip for longer than he needed to, but he always found it difficult to drag his eyes away from the satin sheen of her skin. His desire to stroke it alarmed him, especially as he had recently noticed his increasing tendency to be impulsive. So far he had explained this to himself as the early onset of a mid-life crisis, for which he blamed Kate.

"Tulip, you were going to prepare a report for us on Bradley Hicks."

"Yes. I saw Bradley again on Monday. I noticed several new marks on his body – cuts, scratches and bruises. However, according to Mrs Hicks, Mr Hicks had already been away working for almost three weeks, so any suspicion that his father was physically abusing him would seem to be eliminated. At this stage we cannot rule out that his mother may be responsible. She has often been very short-tempered with the children when I am there. She admits to being stressed a lot of the time but denies hitting the children other than an occasional slap on the arm or leg. Bradley's injuries, however, are all over his body. His younger brother Leonardo, who at six years old is a year younger than Bradley, has no marks on him at all. Both boys confirm their mother's story."

"How long did you say that this family has been on our books?"

"Three months. A neighbour reported hearing regular shouting, screaming and crying and that one of the children seemed to have constant injuries."

"What are your conclusions and recommendations?"

"So far I have no clear conclusions. According to his parents Bradley is a far more active child than his brother and often comes home with marks on him that they claim he didn't have when he went out, though the boy is unwilling or unable to explain how he came by them. His parents say he sneaks out of the house without permission and may not return for a couple of hours or more. Neighbouring children confirm that they often see Bradley out and about with a group of older boys. It may be that they know something about the marks on Bradley, but they haven't been identified yet. This possibility is supported by the fact that Bradley has injuries and Leonardo does not, but we know that it is sometimes only one particular child in a family who gets abused. My recommendation is that this family should stay on our books for another six months at least for further investigations, during which time I will continue to make weekly visits and try to establish the source of Bradley's injuries."

"Thank you, Tulip. Has anyone any comments?"

74

A stocky middle-aged man cleared his throat. David braced himself, ready to bite his tongue in the face of what Cliff might say. He didn't consider Cliff particularly suited to social work.

"Surely we should be considering the possibility of taking Bradley into care since he seems clearly at risk? After all at only seven years old he is very vulnerable and may be afraid to contest his parents' stories. We don't want this to be one of those cases where no action is taken until it's too late."

"I think that's unlikely to happen," said Tulip. "At the moment there's no concrete evidence that he's being abused. An occasional slap on the arm or leg doesn't constitute abuse, although I am aware that the law could change on that. Bradley actually seems quite a happy kid, the injuries are not too serious and could be sustained by trying to keep up with the older kids and trying to do what they do."

"That doesn't prove anything. How many more tragedies have to occur before we take the correct preventative action? And if he regularly goes out without permission are the parents exercising an appropriate level of control? If not then the children are at risk anyway."

David sighed. "There's really not enough evidence so far that it's necessary, Cliff. I'm happy to leave it to Tulip to get further information. Tulip, since you are seeing the family again next week perhaps you could broach the issue of control and see what you can do to help the parents address it and report back to me."

"With all due respect to Tulip, what's acceptable in this country is different from what's acceptable where she comes from."

It was only his familiarity with Cliff's obtuseness that prevented David from blowing his top.

"Are you questioning Tulip's professional standards?" he asked icily.

"Not at all," said Cliff, realising his gaff.

"A good hiding never did me any harm," said Tulip cheerfully. "I got a few from my grandmother as well as from my parents. But I can assure you that I am aware of the cultural differences and I am following the recommended professional guidelines for this country."

"Sorry, Tulip. I withdraw my remark," muttered Cliff.

David wasn't going to openly accuse Cliff of racism at this point. He noticed that Tracy was looking at Tulip and grinning. He also noticed that the hem of Tracy's skirt had somehow travelled some way up her thighs. She certainly had less class than Tulip, but was obviously more available. Tracy, he realised, was leading him into areas of serious indiscretion. He would get someone else to give her a lift home tonight, after the group's usual visit to the pub.

Indiscretions and affairs were as common in these offices as in any others, but David had been mortified to find himself behaving in a way which he had always looked down on as being deplorable. Last week he had somehow ended up kissing Tracy in the car outside her house with his hand under her skirt, somewhere in the region of her buttocks. Worse still, he had a suspicion that Sid the milkman might have seen them together in the early hours of the morning at least once, possibly more often, and gossip spread like wildfire in their small community. A cloud of gloom suddenly engulfed him as he remembered with poignancy the intense love he had felt for Kate in the early days, and he was overcome by a longing for the kind of family life he had anticipated when he and Kate were first married.

"David, are you all right?"

He started out of his reverie. It had been Tulip who had spoken.

"Yes. I'm fine."

"Are you sure? You look as though you're going to cry."

David laughed shakily...."No, no, things aren't quite that bad yet, not even in this department."

The reason David had started the Friday evening meetings was to avoid Quentin. During the week Quentin left very early in the morning for the one and a half hour

77

drive to Oxford to deliver his lectures and to check out his temporarily unoccupied flat, or to catch the train to London, and most evenings either came home very late or spent the time working, reading or watching television in his room. On Fridays, though, Quentin was home by mid-afternoon while David was still at work, and often took advantage of this by spending time with Kate and the twins, but this had sometimes extended into Friday evening after David's return from the office. David, resentful of Quentin's relationship with Kate, thought Quentin should behave more like a lodger and keep a respectful distance. This was of course unrealistic, unreasonable even, in view of Quentin's shared history with Kate. However David's sulky attitude was that he was being forced out of his own home. He blamed his sense of violation on Quentin and Kate equally, although he was forced to admit that in the case of Kate at least The Grange was legally her home. On the days when divorce seemed a good idea he thought that to complain to the court of her concern for Quentin's welfare before his, David's, would weigh things in his favour. Her wish to allow Quentin to stay was driving him, David, out of his own home.

David had found that arranging a Friday evening meeting and going to the pub afterwards was a very agreeable solution, and at first didn't admit to himself how much he enjoyed it. He was being forced out by an intruder in his family life, wasn't he? Neither did he admit how much he liked the way the women flirted once in the pub. But after all there had to be some carrot to lure them out to a Friday evening work meeting. The two problems were that Quentin was increasingly filling the vacuum that he, David, left, and Tracy. David's mistake was being brought into sharp focus by the compromising situation in which he now found himself. He didn't even particularly fancy Tracy. In realising this he also realised that he didn't really want a divorce. He could see that the answer was to drop Tracy before he got in any deeper, stop sulking in the role of wronged husband and re-establish himself as the dominant male in the household. However the way things were at the moment between himself and Kate meant that to ask Quentin to leave was going to alienate her still further. He was going to have to bite the bullet and compete for his own wife. He was going to have to start courting her again, or maybe lose her.

Chapter 12

Susan, enveloped in an overlarge cape, was sitting in one of the chairs in Mikey's unisex salon. In the mirror she watched Wendy, who was standing behind her, run her fingers through her, Susan's, hair several times and, holding it out sideways, study it carefully. The shoulder length hair was thick and luxuriant.

"You've got beautiful hair. How do you want it? You haven't had it cut for a while, have you?"

"I've been growing it, but now I've changed my mind. I want it short." Susan spoke quietly, almost shyly.

"How short, and what sort of short?"

The child sitting in front of her was small for her age, which somehow made Wendy feel protective towards her, and she felt herself mellowing towards Susan. Maybe she wasn't a brash brat at all – in the street the girl seemed defiant and full of attitude, but here she seemed softer, more vulnerable.

"I want exactly the same style as the girl across the road."

"What style's that?" asked Wendy, although she knew the answer perfectly well, since she realised to whom Susan was referring.

"D' you know Chloe Dawson? She has her hair cut here."

"Sure I know Chloe."

"Well, that's how I want my hair. Exactly the same as hers."

"Well, that's a compliment to her. You must really like the way she looks."

"I don't give a shit about her or the way she looks. I just want the same hair style. It's her brother I like if you really want to know, not her."

Brash brat after all, thought Wendy.

"What's your mother going to say? I'll have to cut ever such a lot off."

"She won't care."

No, I don't suppose she will," thought Wendy.

Chloe's natty little hair style was cut close to her head at the back and sides but longer on top, especially at the front, a style generally known as 'gamine'. It was well suited to her regular features and was young and sophisticated at the same time. Susan thought that if she looked more like Chloe then Chloe herself, but also and more importantly Jack, might start to like her. She hadn't meant what she said about Chloe but had felt like shocking Wendy a bit. She had every intention of being friendly with Chloe. However most of Susan's waking thoughts were wound around Jack now, particularly since the occasion when he had caught her spying through the garden fence. Susan felt embarrassed about what she had done and didn't even know why she had done it.

"I'll just wash your hair first. Best to cut it wet I think, I won't do the short bits really short this time, just short enough to see if you like it."

Wendy snipped away asking the usual mundane hairdresser questions, and got typical schoolchild monosyllabic answers. Meanwhile Susan's eyes wandered round the salon. The shelves held a huge array of products – shampoos, conditioners, straighteners, moisturisers, shine enhancers and so on. They were all very expensive. No wonder her mother was always so short of money if just taking care of her hair cost so much. But what really fascinated Susan were the posters. It wasn't just the hair of the models, but their glossy lips, perfect complexions and overall Cindy doll appearance. That's how Mum looks, she mused – like a doll. In her mind she pictured her mother at the dressing table mirror for anything up to an hour at a time, surrounded by a sea of lipsticks, eye shadows, mascaras and tinted foundations.

"I don't want to be beautiful," she said aloud. "I want to be a real person with a real life."

At that moment Mikey was walking behind her chair.

"Good for you," he said, "but maybe you're going to be both."

Chapter 13

"And plié, and up ... that's *beautiful*, Chloe. Straighten up, Lucinda, don't lean forward ... and third, heel down – turn that left foot *out*, please, Amy – that's better, and up. Curve that elbow, Pandora, relax those fingers ... and up, and fifth, *point that toe, Naomi* ... plié ... wrists, everyone, wrists ... and now back down to first."

Enraptured, transported, Chloe felt her whole body blending with the music, her torso, limbs, head and breathing in total obedience to its rhythm. She knew of no other sensation in life to equal the exhilaration of it. As the dancers relaxed for a moment after the plié exercise an enormous energy pulsed through her from the top of her head to the soles of her feet. It was never until the end of the class that this sense of total physical power subsided and gave way to a heavy, immobilising tiredness.

The twenty minutes in the changing room before the class began was always a Babylonian hubbub of excited, gossiping little girls, each raising her voice minute by minute in an effort to be heard above the others. Meanwhile they struggled into their leotards and carefully wound the ribbons of their ballet shoes round their ankles until Miss Maidens, the dancing teacher, could no longer stand the din and came in and clapped her hands loudly. The racket subsided instantly because they saw, rather than heard, her do it.

Chloe had almost been late for class. Her parents had been arguing over the arrangements about who was going to have the car at which times, and she had stood there, as usual, feeling tense and powerless. She had changed alone in an empty changing room and scrambled into position at the barre just as Miss Dent was playing the opening chords. Consequently she had not had time to have her usual chat with Naomi.

"Why were you late?" asked Naomi after the class, as they sat on the bench unwinding the ribbons on their shoes.

"Parental argument".

"Again?"

Chloe's head drooped and Naomi wished she'd held her tongue. She'd noticed Chloe becoming more withdrawn over the last few months, and had found out that the Dawson parents weren't getting on. She changed the subject quickly.

"Do you know if my mum phoned your mum this morning?"

"No. I've no idea. Why?"

"My mum's trying to arrange to go away for the weekend with her boyfriend, the weekend of the eighteenth. She's fixed up for my sister to go and stay with a friend and she thought that maybe I could come and stay with you."

Chloe brightened. "That would be cool. The only thing is we've got this relative person coming to stay, but I think that's this coming weekend. She's called Natasha. I'm not sure that Mum's all that keen, but she's coming anyway."

"Who is Natasha?"

"Mum's stepfather's granddaughter by a previous marriage."

"Excuse me?"

Chloe tried again. "Mum's got a step-sister called Daphne. Daphne's father married Mum's mother when Mum was ten and Daphne was nineteen." She paused to give Naomi time to make sense of it so far.

"OK? Well, Natasha is Daphne's daughter, OK?"

"Just about. Why is you Mum letting her come if she doesn't like her?"

"She doesn't exactly not like her. I don't know if she's even ever met her. But she can't stand Daphne, and I don't think they've spoken to each other for about fifteen years. I suppose she thinks Natasha may have turned out like her mother. Daphne was horrid to Mum when she was a child, but Mum says it's not Natasha's fault so she's keeping an open mind."

86

"Well, my mum says your mum owes her one, so I hope I can come. It's great at your house, everyone's so weird. Nice weird," she added hastily.

"It's mostly Quentin actually," said Chloe, but she was more gratified than offended. Unlike Jack, who still needed to conform, Chloe had moved on to the stage of liking being different. If The Grange had been in a more salubrious area it would have been beyond the reach of the Dawsons financially, and the theatrical side of Chloe adored living in a big house which was grand but a bit shabby at the same time.

"Quentin's really cool," said Naomi. "Is he an actor?"

This made Chloe laugh, much to Naomi's relief – for a moment Chloe was like her old self.

"No, but I know what you mean. He behaves like one sometimes. Jack and I like him too. So does Mum."

"What about your dad?"

"I don't think they really like each other, but Quentin's and old friend of Mum's, so there's not much he can do about it really."

"Do you think that's what they argue about so much?"

"I don't think so. They haven't been getting on for ages." Her voice wobbled. "I hate it. I'm scared."

Naomi put her arm round her friend. "It'll be OK. My parents split up didn't they? And I'm all right, aren't I? I was scared too, but now it's much better than it was before they split up and rowed all the time."

"It's not just that. There's Jack as well."

"What about Jack?"

"There's a girl who's after him and I can't stand her, she's as common as muck and so is her mother."

"Why does it matter? You've been saying lately that Jack is babyish and boring and you're glad you don't have to spend so much time with him anymore."

"I want him to grow up and start doing worthwhile things. That doesn't mean I want him hijacked by some common little tart in the meantime. He's my brother, my *twin* brother, and I'm not having him being taken over by somebody else."

"Who is this girl?"

"She lives opposite us. They've just moved in."

Naomi's eyes lit up.

"Persuade your mother to let me come and stay no matter what. We'll go and visit this girl and sort her out."

Chapter 14

"More wine?"

"Please."

Quentin refilled Ursula's glass and then his own. She picked up the drink and looked down into it thoughtfully.

"The thing is, Quentin, you really mustn't expose yourself to any more emotional trauma. Suppose all the feelings come back when you see him again? I think Kate was very foolish to invite him."

Quentin was gazing at her upper lip, wondering why her moustache was so much more noticeable in the subdued lighting of the restaurant than it was in daylight.

Ursula sensed, and hoped, that Quentin was looking at her. She had treated herself to a new lipstick – new both in the sense that she had only just bought it, and also in the sense that she had never before bought any shade other than Pillar Box Red, of which she always had half a dozen or so sticks at any one time and which she considered eminently suitable for work. Until now she wouldn't have bothered with lipstick at all except for the fact that she considered an unmade-up face unprofessional as far as her job was concerned. Tonight, however, she was wearing a colour called Caribbean Coral in wet gloss texture. She thought it would appeal to Quentin more than the shimmer texture. Her belief that Quentin was capable of any response at all to lipstick was witness to the fact that Ursula had taken leave of her senses.

Ursula had fallen in love.

It had happened very suddenly. She had had feelings of deepening affection for Quentin for some time, but had kept it hidden partly because she wanted to keep their relationship totally professional and partly for fear of ridicule or teasing. Consequently not a soul had the slightest suspicion that she was besotted with the self-absorbed neurotic sitting opposite her, his newly-washed blonde curls gleaming, his long fingers with the immaculately buffed nails curled around the stem of his glass.

Ursula had been concerned about Quentin during the last three years, and was much relieved that he now appeared to have regained his equilibrium. At one time she wouldn't have been remotely interested in his welfare. When she had first encountered him almost twelve years previously she hadn't liked him at all. A PhD, a couple of well-received papers and four years of lecturing behind him, and just before the start of his narcissistic relationship with Simon, he had come across as rude and contemptuous.

"Cocky little man," she had commented disparagingly to a fellow student at Oxford. But because Quentin, naturally, used libraries a lot, when Ursula took up her post at the British Library in London they began seeing a good deal of each other. Their professional rapport blossomed and Ursula, having first witnessed from a distance, during her own undergraduate years, the birth of Quentin's relationship with Simon, then watched its subsequent crumbling, together with the devastation of a massive ego.

It was over three years ago that Quentin had started to become quiet and morose. He would stare into space for minutes at a time. He lost his dapper appearance and began to look crumpled and dowdy. Eventually Ursula ventured to ask him if he was all right, and the flood gates had opened. Quentin had been unable to confide in Kate because of her own relationship with Simon, and now it had become impossible to bottle it all up. Ursula came to hear in minute detail and with a good deal of repetition the unlikely story of Quentin's love for the beautiful young student many years his junior and its increasing lack of productivity and was asked, pitifully, for a prognosis. She had never met Simon herself so she had no direct observation of her own to go on.

It was the exposing of Quentin's vulnerability that had touched Ursula's heart. Her own lack of romantic associations belied her capacity for compassion, and she found herself wishing for the return of his former obnoxious personality rather than have to endure the sight of this pathetic, demoralised creature. As the weeks passed she became almost as desperate as he was.

The day arrived when he came, pale and stooping, into the Library looking so ill that she hardly recognised him. He sat looking blankly in front of him for hours, until the Library was about to close. He was like a man in a trance, and put up no resistance when Ursula took him by the arm and gently led him back to his hotel room. When she visited him a couple of days later, once he was able to speak again, he told her that he had been, effectively, dumped. Simon had informed him by telephone that he wanted no contact for a year. He had said that he needed to concentrate on his work and wanted total solitude with no distractions. Quentin feared this to be terminal, irretrievable. He had sensed it coming for months, but had been hoping that he was imagining it.

The practical Ursula immediately took control of the situation and steered Quentin into a total change in his life that would provide an exclusive and relentless focus. This, they quickly decided, should take the form of a sabbatical year and a new publication. The University was shortly going down for the summer. A hasty conference with the Dean confirmed that teaching cover could be arranged. Together Quentin and Ursula chose a topic for his paper and began researching it immediately, even before his sabbatical officially began, because Ursula had understood the importance of filling to capacity all his waking hours. She kept him mercilessly occupied, mostly researching with deadlines imposed by herself, although sometimes they relaxed over a meal together or made a very occasional visit to the theatre or cinema. For good measure Ursula made

Quentin promise faithfully that he would make no attempt of any kind to contact Simon.

She had thought that it had worked. By the time his sabbatical year was over although the paper was nowhere near ready the obsession seemed to have faded, and Quentin told Ursula that he realised that he had made a complete fool of himself and was preparing himself to make a formal and dignified exit from Simon's life with a calm and rational telephone call.

"Why bother to phone him at all? After all it's been a year now and he hasn't contacted you. Why not just let it go?"

"Because I need closure. Without an official termination the thing's still open. All it needs is a simple phone call."

That, he had said, would be the end of the matter. He had meant it. He had believed it. Ursula intuitively felt that this reasoning was flawed, but not being a particularly emotional person she couldn't quite put her finger on why.

Cunningly, treacherously, self-delusion was already reasserting itself. The old-style Quentin was already beginning to re-form and consolidate. The new paper, though not finished, had been shaping up rather well, and Quentin Montague, Oxford University Senior Lecturer, had begun to anticipate becoming Quentin Montague, Oxford

University Reader. Brimming with the confidence bestowed by this idea he had picked up the phone to make the fatal call. For some reason it surprised him that Simon actually answered. Instantly the thumping heart, churning stomach, and weak feeling in his knees returned. For a minute or two he thought he was having a heart attack. Caught off-guard, face-saving mechanically, Quentin told Simon that he respected his need to focus on his work and that he, Quentin, had the same need due to a new paper in the pipeline, so although the year of seclusion that Simon had requested had expired he himself was now in need of the same and unable to keep in touch for the time being. Simon offered no protest but wished Quentin well with the writing of his paper.

When Quentin put down the phone he was shaking like a leaf. The sound of Simon's voice, distant, cool, polite, had pressed a button in him. The obsession was back, the addiction renewed, the rejection confirmed. He had felt terrible. He hadn't known where to turn. Ursula? Kate? No, he couldn't face them. Until this new crisis was over he would have to somehow hold down the lecturing job to which he was about to return and cope on his own. And so he had for over a year, with the help of substantial quantities of alcohol, tobacco and marijuana, until these three took him over and Kate took him in. He gave her the perennial excuse that it was pressure of work that had wrought this havoc in him, and since she knew that he was indeed working very hard and thought he had got over Simon, she believed him.

The restorative effect of family life with the Dawsons had enabled Quentin to continue with his old job by the time the new autumn term arrived. By Christmas he was back working on his Oxfordshire village house project, delivering sparkling lectures, enjoying living with the Dawsons apart from the presence of David and at last back working with Ursula on the final details of his paper. Kate and Ursula, who by now were on quite friendly terms with each other, were cautiously congratulating themselves on a satisfactory outcome to what had seemed a hopeless situation. They believed that apart from the phone call of 'closure' a year and a half previously, which they assumed had been successful, Quentin had had nothing to do with Simon for two and a half years. Kate had said a few months later, rather petulantly, that it hadn't occurred to her to consult Ursula on the question of whether or not it would be advisable to invite Simon to the Queen's Golden Jubilee street party. She insisted no, she didn't think Quentin's constant talking about this coming event and the recurrence of his moody behaviour was anything to do with Simon, or excitement at the idea of seeing Simon again. And since Simon was a dear friend of her own, of several years' standing now, of course she was bound to invite him, given that all risk to Quentin seemed to be over. Some would have agreed with David, that is to say that Kate was something of a control freak, playing the amateur social worker-cum-psychologist, thinking as she did that a meeting between the two of them would confirm and consolidate Quentin's cure as well as renew a worthwhile friendship. Kate knew that all she had in mind, however mistakenly, was the welfare of two dear friends and her desire to share a happy occasion with them both.

But of course unknown to Quentin's nearest and dearest, the delusion that he could win Simon round was still there, and now Ursula, gazing into Quentin's eyes over her glass of wine, was developing fantasies of her own.

Chapter 15

"Come on now, lads – let's get closed up, now." Stan, the proprietor of Blues, was ready to shoo them out and shut up shop.

Joe and Alan took one last shot each then unscrewed their cues and put them in their cases.

"Walk round the long way with me?" asked Joe. "The long way for you, that is!" He laughed.

"Sure." It actually suited Alan fine, on this particular night, to draw out his journey home by accompanying Joe to Cannon Street and then doubling back up Muller Road.

Joe's most direct way home lay past the Oak Leaf, the pub where his natural parents drank, and he preferred not to go that way unless he had someone with him. It wasn't that he was still afraid of them, not in the same way. Now that he was pretty much full grown and eighteen years old there was little chance of them physically assaulting him and none at all of them being able to take him back. But when they saw him they approached with gushing sentimentality, saying how they missed him and worried about him, asking if he was all right and whether he was being properly fed and well-treated. This repelled and embarrassed him. Once or twice they had asked him for money, which he had never given them. Then there ensued a torrent of abuse on the subject of his meanness and his indifference to the welfare of his own parents.

"I suppose you're too good for us now," they said. "How can you turn your back on your own parents? You've got no natural feelings you 'aven't, leaving your own flesh and blood in the gutter."

Joe knew that Mikey was right. Even if he did give them money they couldn't benefit from it - it would simply get spent on more booze. He knew that there was no way in which he could help his parents, or they him. Yet however often he thought it through a conflict remained in his mind. He could not stop himself wanting to help them, wanting them to change, wanting them to be happy. It was easier if, when he encountered them, he was not alone.

Joe had no sense of shame or obligation regarding Arthur and Maud. Mikey had been working on him for eleven years, and Joe understood that he was responsible for no one's behaviour other than his own, that Arthur and Maud had treated him badly because they were sick, not because they didn't love him. Some of his friends had problems in their own families –pregnant under age sisters, divorced parents, fathers in prison or out of work, or drunken parents of their own. Joe knew that life is difficult and judgement rarely helpful or appropriate.

By the time Joe and Alan were outside the Oak Leaf most of the punters had dispersed. It was a good half hour after closing time. There was no sign of Arthur or Maud. Joe suddenly realised that after a good ten minutes of walking the normally chatty Alan hadn't said a word.

"Cat got ya tongue?"

"Maybe."

"You're very quiet."

Silence. Then, "Maybe I got something on me mind."

"Like what?"

"Like a girl."

"*Aha!* In love, eh? Who is she?"

"I don't know her name. I've only seen her."

"Oh no! Dodgy, man."

"She isn't."

"Where did you meet her? See her I mean."

"The Dugout."

"Oh, man. Worse and worse."

"Lay off, Joey. It's serious. Tell you what, why don't we go down there now, maybe I can point her out."

Joe sighed.

"Go on, please, Joey. We don't need to stay long."

Joe thought for a moment. Mikey would be playing tonight. A year ago Joe wouldn't have dared to go as Mikey would not have wanted to see him there, especially at this hour, but although nothing had specifically been said Joe knew that he was now his own boss, trusted to make his own decisions. In fact quite unexpectedly Mikey had recently suggested that he might like to 'come down and listen to the music, especially on a Friday'. Joe was tired and would have preferred to go home to bed, but Alan was his friend.

"C'mon then, buddy," he said, "Let's go."

Chapter 16

Sheila followed Natasha up the steps and through the door of the ticket office. Natasha turned and smiled. They embraced. Bill the Ticket moved away from his window and fiddled with his ticket machine.

"Good luck."

"You too."

They felt like sisters but were not. Each was embarking on what could be a life-changing journey. Each understood the significance of the expedition of the other. They disentangled themselves.

"Bristol Temple Meads please Bill," said Natasha, though her tongue still wanted to say "Taunton please Bill", as it had for the last ten years at the beginning of every train journey she and her brother Raj had taken on their own since she was eight and he was twelve. These had been the few occasions when neither of their parents had been available to drive them down from Worcestershire to their school in Somerset. Her use of Foregate Street Station was likely to be just as frequent now that her schooldays were over and her university days soon to begin. Her father had wanted to buy her a car for her eighteenth birthday, but she had refused his indulgent offer. She wanted a typical student experience and did not want to stand out as wealthy – she knew her father was not thinking of buying her an old banger.

The man at the window smiled at her. Natasha had grown into a rare, dark Anglo-Indian beauty, and Bill was entranced to see how the gentle, polite little girl he had known since she was old enough to go away and be a weekly boarder had become a poised, sweet-natured young lady. They were long-time friends.

"That's a new one. Schooldays over, then?"

She smiled back. "Yes. It feels strange. Part of me wants to turn the clock back and another part wants to move on."

"You'll get used to it. There's grand times ahead for you I'll be bound, a bright lass like you."

So different from her mother, he thought. He felt sorry for Daphne for all her wealth and high social status, whose crippling snobbery, inherited from her father, kept her tense, vulnerable and unhappy.

Bill turned to Sheila. "How about you, Miss? Where're you off to?"

"Sherborne please, Bill." The ticket machine whirred again.

"There you go, m' dear. Same train as Natasha to start with. Change at Bristol Temple Meads when Natasha gets off."

Ensconced in her seat, watching the late spring countryside flitting past, Natasha slipped into a comfortable reverie. She thought of Nanny Barbara who had soothed and nurtured her through her early years. Her father, Rachit, didn't really approve of nannies, especially in the case of the children of non-working mothers who had plenty of domestic help, but he came to see what a blessing Nanny Barbara was to Raj and Natasha. Natasha thought of her schooldays at Queens College, where she and Raj had both thrived. She thought of her mother, whom she loved in spite of the near impossibility of engaging with her. Daphne was the immutable product of her aristocratic background and its hugely outdated priorities, which automatically included employing someone else to have the day to day care of one's children. Natasha thought of her adored racehorse owner father and of the wonderful outdoor life he had encouraged her and Raj to live. He was the person Natasha loved best. The three of them had spent most of their leisure time out riding and going to polo matches, horse races, three-day events and gymkhanas.

She looked affectionately across at Sheila, whom her parents had all but adopted when Sheila's family situation had become stressful. Right now Sheila had her head buried in an interior design magazine. A year ago it would have been more likely to have been Horse and Hound, but a recent accident looked like it was going to put an end to Sheila's horse-riding career. Sheila it had been who, at the age of eleven, had helped show three-year-old Natasha how to ride – firstly on Bunty the Shetland and later on all Natasha's other ponies and horses. Sheila it had been who had eventually coached Natasha and Magic Carpet to victory at the junior show jumping at the Horse of the Year show.

Sheila had never had a pony of her own. Her parents could not have afforded it. From childhood and through adolescence she had earned riding lessons by helping out at the local stables. She had followed the local hunt on foot, eagerly watched show jumping and eventing on television, joined the pony club and gone to endless lengths to increase her knowledge of horses and improve her riding. She sometimes took part in small local events on riding school ponies and horses. Rachit had expressed his gratitude for her efforts with his daughter by helping Sheila open her own riding school – her own parents didn't have the means. Now, however, Sheila was selling up the riding school and planned to use the proceeds to pay for a course in interior design and set up a consultancy.

Natasha was primarily going to Bristol to see if she liked the place, because if she did she was intending to go to university there. She had already secured a provisional offer which she would accept if she got the required examination grades. Her parents thought she just wanted it for backup purposes in the event that she did not succeed in the Oxford entrance examinations which, theoretically, she would sit in the autumn. She had not told them that if her exam results were good enough for Bristol she would go there immediately and not sit the Oxbridge exams at all. Natasha knew Oxford well. Both her parents had gone there and Raj was there now, but, maybe as a reaction to her mother's suffocating aspirations, Natasha secretly wanted to go somewhere a bit less high profile as well as be more assertive about her own choices.

The intriguing part of Natasha's trip was that Daphne had arranged for her to stay for a few days with some relatives whom Natasha would be meeting for the very first time, in particular a step aunt about whom she had heard from her mother. Natasha had learned years ago to ignore, or at least edit, whatever Daphne said, so she didn't really know what to expect when she got to the Dawson's. That is to say, although she took Daphne's word for it that Kate was indeed thirty-seven years old, the mother of eleven-year-old twins (a girl and a boy), married and a housewife, she doubted that she was of low intelligence and somewhat sulky, frumpy and inarticulate. Fond of her mother and charitable by nature Natasha was keeping an open mind about these unknown relatives.

Sheila was going to Dorset to visit her only brother again in the wake of their recent reconciliation. Prior to that she hadn't seen him at all for eleven years. She had been only fourteen when he had gone off under a cloud to study at Oxford University, leaving her baffled, anxious, upset. He had never gone back home or ever tried to make contact with his parents or sister. At the time no one had told Sheila what it was all about, and she had been afraid to ask. She knew it had something to do with her friend Denise, but she had never seen Denise again until last year. A week after the incident (Sheila had been aware that there had *been* an incident), the GCSE examinations over, Denise and her family had moved to a different part of the country in connection with her father's job. On the surface family life had gone on without Simon as though he had never existed, as though nothing had happened. The main routine of Sheila's life was still in place – home, school, parents and friends and, thankfully, the horse-centred activities she enjoyed with the Singh family. Under the surface lurked tension, secrecy, mistrust.

It was over a year after Simon's departure that, through the grapevine, Sheila obtained a distorted account of what had happened. It hurt her deeply, though less so than it would have at the time when she was still in daily contact with her brother. She was also disgusted, and felt that she never wanted to see him again. She didn't admit to anyone that she missed him.

Simon, however, was not going to let his sister go easily – they had been very close until that hot summer's day. He had realised, though, that getting her back might take a considerable amount of time.

He had used her eighteenth birthday for his initial attempt at re-establishing contact with her and had sent her six beautifully drawn pencil sketches of horses. They had captivated her. She allowed herself to send him a brief note of thanks. For the next six years he had regularly sent her birthday and Christmas gifts. Each time she responded a little bit more fully, and a desire to be reunited with Simon was building in her. She wondered if she had been told the truth about what he had done. If he was such a monster why was he being so sweet –as he always had been in the past? Eventually, towards the end of the intervening period, Sheila had encountered Denise, who had come back on a few days' visit to contact old friends. At first, when asked, Denise was unable to remember any particular event involving herself and Sheila's brother. When it came back to her after some tearful prompting from Sheila she laughed.

"Oh, that! It was nothing. I should probably have taken better advantage of it – a hunk like your brother, wow! The thing was, he made me jump and I screamed. The neighbours came running over, I ran off, and after that I really can't remember much more, though I've an idea that the whole thing got blown up out of all proportion in people's minds."

Denise, by this time pursuing a relationship with a body builder that was nothing if not carnal, would have been horrified had she known the extent of the effect the incident had had on Simon, Sheila and their parents.

Rumour had it that when Simon was only two or three years old mesmerised little girls would approach him at nursery, in the park or on the beach and want to touch him. At school, by the time he was seven, he was always the first choice with girls to be on their team or sit next to them in class or at lunch, but it was after this that he really began to feel the pressure. By the time the first term at secondary school had elapsed he was refusing point blank to go to the bike sheds with any girl to see what was wrong with her brakes or why her tyres kept going down. By the time he was fourteen girls he barely knew would knock on the door and ask to speak to him. His fear of girls also somehow made him unable to socialise in a normal way with other boys, most of whom had started dating, or were trying to.

The day came when Denise came round to the Barnes' house one summer afternoon to see Sheila, scantily clad on account of the exceptional heat. Simon, who knew her fairly well, had answered the door. He had invited her in and taken a step backwards to allow her to enter when she tripped on the step. She had fallen against him and somehow the straps had accidently slipped from her shoulders, leaving her naked to the waist. For no reason that he ever understood Simon started kissing her face and neck with unquenchable passion and was working towards her chest when she screamed, chiefly from surprise. She had never been one of those who pursued him romantically, mainly because she had always had more immediate requirements and had correctly assumed that he did not fall into that category. The neighbours, who had been sitting under the cherry tree on their front lawn sipping aperitifs, had come rushing over and separated them. His parents refused to listen to his explanation and made him leave for Oxford a few days later, telling him that they never wished to see or speak to him again.

"It's lucky for you that you're not up on an assault charge," they had said.

"But ... "

"No buts. We'll never be able to hold our heads up in this town again. Don't ever come back."

The story did make a brief appearance in the local paper, but nothing ever came of it.

If it hadn't been for Natasha and her family Sheila might have come seriously unstuck at this time because her parents, though well-meaning, were not particularly bright and hadn't thought about the effect that Simon's disappearance might have on their daughter. Natasha's parents heard the gossip, which became elaborated upon as it passed from mouth to mouth, and to support and distract Sheila they had increasingly asked for her help with Natasha and the ponies. Even Daphne came to accept her as one of the family in spite of Sheila's inauspicious background. Sheila came to have a busy and privileged life – horse riding, visits to point to points and polo matches, tickets to the best London shows, weekends in Paris and Vienna. It took up all her spare time, so it was fortunate that she had no wish to follow in her brother's footsteps academically because there was no time at all to study, and after a few months in the sixth form she had given up school altogether.

By the time Sheila came to be eighteen she was coming to terms with the loss of her brother, and the enchanting horse sketches he sent for her birthday gave her hope that one day they might become reconciled. At the same time Rachit came up with his exciting idea of setting her up in her own stables. She repaid him bit by bit as she got established. He gave freely and without charge of his time and expertise. Sheila's life went from strength to strength until the day a few months ago when with a front foot Joker had caught the top rail of a substantial fixed fence, they had fallen heavily and Sheila had sustained severe injuries. As she convalesced she fell to musing about Simon. Denise's recent explanation about what had really happened had filled her with such relief that she had contacted Simon and asked if she could come and stay with him for a few days, and he had agreed.

Fearful of the fragility of this renewed contact they had both avoided referring to 'the incident', and Simon certainly hadn't told her about Quentin. All the same they had begun the process of becoming reacquainted with each other, and Sheila was feeling both apprehensive and excited as the train to Bristol hurtled through the sunny countryside.

Chapter 17

Sid's cup of happiness was full. As always he had taken his first holiday of the year at the beginning of May to give himself the opportunity, weather permitting, of getting the garden off to a good start. Every morning he got up early to make the most of the day.

The weather this year had been changeable at best, but today was glorious. The delicious freshness and faint mist of the early morning had given way to a clear, bottomless quietness that was beginning to melt into a bright, penetrating warmth. He pottered around his greenhouse looking to see what had come into bud, what into flower, what needed watering, what needed feeding, what needed repotting. As he worked he sang in his beautiful baritone voice:

> *Morning has broken like the first morning,*
> *Blackbird has spoken like the first bird,*
> *Praise for the singing, praise for the morning,*
> *Both of them springing fresh from the Word.*

The door and windows of the greenhouse were wide open, but the breeze that gently wafted through made no impact on the perfume hanging in the air, which became daily thicker and heavier as more and more blooms opened their petals to reveal their innermost secrets. Some of these plants were for the adornment of his own garden, but at the far end of the greenhouse there was a whole section containing plants that were barely in bud. The precise timing of these, especially the freesias, was paramount.

There was a month to go to the street party. Sid studied the freesias intently and most of them, if you looked carefully, were just putting out the tiniest of buds, barely bigger than pin pricks. Perfect. He should now be able to get them just right. Kate hadn't specified freesias, nor were these the only flowers that Sid was planning on supplying. He had roses, carnations, delphiniums and others all lined up ready, according to which of them had reached exactly the right stage to be ready on the big day, to compete for a place alongside the freesias on the street party table. But he knew freesias were Kate's favourite and he wanted to surprise her.

Out of the corner of his eye Sid was watching Jack Dawson loitering on the other side of the hedge at the bottom of the garden, watching him. The boy was obviously bored, and Sid was trying to decide whether or not to invite him in for a glass of lemonade. He thought he might since Wendy, as usual, was drinking tea in Kathleen's kitchen.

Jack was indeed a bit fed up, but less so than he might have been. Chloe had gone off once more, to the London theatre this time with Kate and the rest of her dancing class and their mothers to see The Nutcracker, and Jack's attempts at independence were still rather faltering. He'd been left on his own again in the care of his father who, to his astonishment (as well as Chloe's and Kate's), had offered to take him to a cricket match at the County Ground later that day, after he had finished writing a report for work. Better still, David had said that they could go every Saturday afternoon throughout the summer when he was available. David's resolve to oust Quentin as the most popular man in the family was in earnest.

Jack was thrilled to be going to a sporting event with his father. Not only would there be some well-known cricketers playing, but the mere fact of David doing a man thing with him, just the two of them, was unheard of, and Jack felt special and important. But it seemed a long time to wait till lunchtime, and as usual he was having difficulty occupying himself. It was the first May bank holiday weekend and most of his mates were doing things with their families. Computer games were only available to Jack at his friends' houses, because although the Dawsons had finally acquired a computer Kate and David disapproved of computer games and didn't allow them. Jack had temporarily lost interest in the rabbits, and though The Grange had a biggish garden it wasn't that good for kicking a ball around in, what with all the bushes and everything. Anyhow he was a bit apprehensive of going into the garden alone for any length of time, because he was beginning to think that the girl over the road (he knew by now that her name was Susan) was spying on them – or on him. In fact it was obvious that she was, because two or three times now he'd seen her crouching in the bushes on the path which ran alongside their garden, peering at them from among the leaves, and finally last Sunday there had been that morning when she had stood right up against the fence, bold as you like, with her blouse unbuttoned down the front and her naked chest, the details of which he had been too aghast to fully register, revealed. He had run inside quickly and cannoned into his father in the kitchen, who had said,

"What on earth's the matter?" to which Jack had mumbled,

"Nothing", and careered straight on up to his bedroom and slammed the door. A moment later, looking out of his bedroom window, he had seen David go out into the garden and look towards the path, but whether or not he saw what he himself had seen Jack was not able to discover. Jack had been feeling anxious and preoccupied since this event, thinking about Susan a lot and feeling both repelled by and attracted to her. Watching ordinary old Sid working in his ordinary old greenhouse and listening to his singing was somehow awfully reassuring.

Eventually Sid went to the door of the greenhouse and called out: "Fancy a glass of lemonade, young Jack?"

"Yes, please."

They sat on the back doorstep to drink it.

"Haven't you got anything to do, then?" asked Sid.

"No."

"Friends all away, are they?"

"Yes."

"Where's yer sister?"

"Gone to the ballet with Mum."

"I must say I thought it was a bit quiet round here this morning," said Sid. "But it's bank holiday weekend, isn't it? A lot of folk go away, don't they? The little lass over the way's still here, though, I saw her a few minutes ago, going in the direction of her house, though it could've been your house seeing as you live opposite. Friend of yours, is she? I know she's new to the area of course, but it doesn't usually take you kids long to make friends."

"She's a *girl*," said Jack uncomfortably.

"You don't say. So's your sister. Half the people in the world are. Don't you like girls? Never mind, you soon will." He turned and winked at Jack, who felt himself blushing and about to cry.

Then Sid said, "Like flowers, do you?"

Jack had never before thought about whether he liked flowers or not, but immediately realised that he did, rather.

"Yes."

Sid smiled.

"Come and have a look, then – but be sure not to tell anyone what you've seen, 'specially your mother."

"I won't," promised Jack.

Jack learned a lot that morning. Some of the things he remembered from school. He found out about loam and peat, clay soils and sandy soils, root balls and transpiration, pruning and cuttings. He sieved compost and sowed seeds and became totally absorbed in this new activity, and all the while he and Sid sang. They sang every song that either of them could think of that they both knew, and when they didn't sing they chatted.

"You've got a smashing voice, you have," said Sid. "We could do with you in our church choir, that we could."

"Our family doesn't go to church," explained Jack. "We don't believe in it."

"What don't you believe in?" asked Sid.

Jack hesitated.

"I don't know," he said lamely. He didn't like to say they didn't believe in God. As it happened he did believe in God, and he knew Chloe did too, but they hadn't mentioned it to their parents because they didn't think they would like it, especially David. It wasn't so much 'we don't believe in it' as 'they don't believe in it', but Jack didn't want to go into all that stuff now, he had other things to think about. What with Chloe not being there half the time any more, and that awful Susan making his life a misery and the parents rowing all the time he felt as though he had the weight of the world on his shoulders. All the same he decided it would be good to talk to Sid more often.

"I do quite like singing," he offered tentatively.

"Well, you know where to come if you change your mind. Now don't you think you'd better be getting along? You Dad'll be wondering what's happened to you."

Jack came bursting through the door just as David, having finished his report, was putting his papers away.

"Goodness me," he said to his son, startled by Jack's uncustomary ebullience. "What have you been up to?"

"Helping Sid in his greenhouse."

"Oh," said David, at a loss for words. It was hardly a reply he had been expecting, but he was glad to see the boy in an upbeat mood for a change. He had been thinking that Jack had seemed rather withdrawn lately. David had at last started to notice the effect he was having on his children.

Chapter 18

"What's up with you then? Lost a pound and found a shilling?" It wasn't that Kathleen wasn't au fait with contemporary currency, but you can't change a saying.

"That tart's pregnant."

"I beg your pardon?"

"Miss airs and graces over the road. Imogen. She's going to have a baby."

"How d' you know that?"

"The brat came in to make an appointment. She told me."

"Susan?"

"Yes."

Kathleen gave herself a moment or two to absorb this new piece of local gossip, then said,

"I saw Imogen yesterday. Quite warm it was and she had on one of them clingy jersey dresses we saw in White Stuff. She didn't look pregnant to me."

"Well, she's only six weeks, so the girl said. She must have done a test. You couldn't know otherwise, could you?"

"You wouldn't say that if had ever happened to you, m' girl. I always knew the next day m'self, or even straight away."

At this Wendy put her face in her hands and burst into tears.

Kathleen had left school at fourteen with minimal formal education, but when it came to affairs of the heart there was none so knowing. She needed no further explanation from Wendy about her mood.

"What's to stop you and Sid from having one? Could cause a bit of a hiccup in your hairdressing plans p'rhaps, but you could always pick that up again later if you wanted."

"We've been trying for three years." Wendy fished out a tissue and dabbed at her eyes.

"Oh," said Kathleen. "Well they can do something about it these days you know."

"I've suggested going for treatment but Sid hasn't been keen. He says if it's meant to happen it will. And we're not sure if we can afford for me to give up work. I've told him he needs to go on a course and train for a better job but he won't."

Wendy started crying again.

Hormones, thought Kathleen. She had good reason to know about hormones, since her own had led her to giving birth to her first child when she was seventeen, then going on to have five more before they (the hormones) were subdued by the endless round of drudgery and chores, made worse in those days by the lack of fan-assisted cookers, microwave ovens, fully automatic washing machines and nursery schools.

"I agree with Sid m' self. After all you're still in yer twenties."

"Sid's thirty-five."

"Plenty time yet. My friend was trying for eleven years before she had her first. Best thing that could have happened. Gave 'em time to get themselves straight before it all started, and enough money. Not like me, living with bare floorboards and rags for nappies 'cos we had no money."

Wendy blew her nose. "Perhaps you're right. I've got a few years yet. I could start my own salon in a couple of years' time – we've almost got enough money put by, and I could get in people to help, like Mikey does, to run it when I needed to be at home."

"That's the way, my love, it'll all work out, you'll see."

Chapter 19

Whilst Wendy and Kathleen sat drinking tea at Kathleen's kitchen table, Kate and Chloe were eating their ice creams during the interval of The Nutcracker, David and Jack were sitting in the afternoon sunshine at the county ground, munching the snacks that David had purchased at the bar, Sheila and Natasha were sitting on a train speeding towards their destinations and Imogen, Shane and Susan were sitting in the stuffy atmosphere of The Sceptre.

"You look about eighteen with that haircut," said Imogen to Susan. Wendy, intimidated by the contrast with Susan's previous luxuriant mane, had hesitated to cut her hair quite as short as she kept Chloe's, and lacking the gamine quality of Chloe's cut the style made Susan look older. Susan, however, wanted it shorter and more like Chloe's, and had been back to Mikey's to make another appointment.

Susan wasn't sure whether or not her mother was speaking with disapproval, but didn't care. Imogen's opinions didn't count for much with her at the moment as long as there was no danger of going into care again. Susan's agenda was to get in with the Dawson children. She didn't know why she was so attracted to them. The fact was, to her they were fascinating because they were 'different'. Most of the other kids in Susan's life to date had been underprivileged in one way or another, mainly because she and Imogen had always been near the bottom of the social scale themselves. Imogen herself had grown up in a children's home and never had any idea of where her parents were, though she knew their names. She had never felt inspired to look for them nor, seemingly, had they for her. Boys, make-up and clothes had been her main interests from younger than Susan's age, and it was a miracle that she had been as much as nineteen when Susan was born. Susan was a candidate for falling into the same pattern. Like her mother she had always attended schools in the poorest areas. But they now lived in a socially mixed area, and what was different this time was having the Dawsons across the road, as well as a sprinkling of teachers and nurses further down the street inter-dispersed with, among others, casual workers, general labourers, office workers, a museum director, an eye surgeon and a prostitute. The twins were not like any other kids Susan had known. They did unusual things. They played chess. Chloe did ballet. Quentin lived with them, and he was like someone out of a film. The twins and their parents dressed in a style that reminded Susan of the Famous Five (Susan liked to read Enid Blyton stories when there was nothing on television), a thing against which Chloe and Jack were about to rebel had Susan known it, but Susan liked it although at school she sniggered at it along with the other up-to-date kids. David and Quentin had important jobs; they were an 'educated' family. Their lives had a purpose outside of mating and reproduction and acquiring things.

There weren't many other customers in the pub. The doors were locked on this sunny afternoon and only chosen members of the pub's clientele were inside. Some were there because they were big spenders. Road and motorway workers like Norman, Samson and Badger were among these. They were good-natured guys who, by the time they had paid for their food and cheap lodgings, still had three-quarters of their wages left to hand over to whichever pub in which they chose to drink. Amos had known Shane for some time, having gone to school with him years ago. He also had a soft spot for Imogen, mainly because she looked so frail and defenceless.

Susan had finished her coke and was bored. Although, unknown to her mother, she sometimes drank alcohol with her friends she wasn't daft enough to ask for it in the pub, and for all Susan's youth Amos had never questioned her presence. Besides, Susan spent as little time there as possible since she found it so dull.

"Are we going soon?"

"No," said Imogen," we've only just got here."

"You'll have to be careful now, love, about how much you have."

"I'm only six weeks. I've got a bit of time."

"You haven't. The early weeks are the most important."

"Is it all right if I go?" asked Susan, sensing a row.

"No," said Imogen, "sit where you are."

"Course you can, love. Be home by seven. I'm doing a chicken casserole."

"You're taking your time with that pint aren't you?" said Imogen, twirling her empty wine glass by its stem.

"It's only fair for me to slow down since you've got to."

"I haven't got to do anything," snapped Imogen. She drank quite a lot more than Shane as a rule, but this was the first time he had mentioned anything about lifestyle because of the baby. Imogen intended to resist this; she knew all the do's and don'ts anyway, and didn't really believe they made any difference. She had drunk all through her other pregnancy and couldn't see that it had done Susan any harm.

Shane was not afraid to put his foot down.

"It's going to be different for this baby. It's not going to grow up like Susan."

"And what's wrong with Susan?" asked Imogen icily. "I thought you liked her."

"I do. I really like her. That's not what I meant. What I meant was, I don't want this baby to grow up the way Susan has been growing up. I want it to have two parents and a proper family life. I want it to have a secure home and stability. I want us to spend time with it doing kid things, Susan too."

"Can I have another glass of wine, please?" Imogen wasn't going to risk proceeding with this argument until another drink was safely in front of her, for fear that she might otherwise have to forego it.

"Absolutely the last one today," said Shane, standing up and putting her glass on the bar so that Dainty could refill it.

"Don't like to pry," said Dainty as she turned to the wine box on the shelf, "but is someone else going to join Piety in the ranks of mother to be?"

Shane grinned broadly. "Could be."

"Congratulations. This one's on the house. What's yours, Shane?"

Dainty's well-wishing smoothed out Imogen's mood.

"Thanks, Dainty."

"You two gonna be getting married, then?"

"No," said Imogen.

"Yes," said Shane.

"For heaven's sake, hardly anyone gets married these days."

"Lots of people do, actually."

Dainty deftly changed the subject. "You two gonna be here Bank Holiday Monday?"

"Yes, of course," said Imogen.

"No," said Shane. "Why?"

"We're doing a special curry. Mo is coming along to cook it for us."

"Of course we'll be here. What's wrong with you, Shane?"

"I promised Susan I'd take her to the fair, remember?"

"Oh, yes, I'd forgotten. But she doesn't need you to take her to the fair. She can go on her own, or with her friends. We don't need to go with her."

"Not true. We never do anything with her and it's not right. Kids need to have grown-ups in their lives to do stuff with them."

"Nobody did with me."

"No. And it shows. And it's beginning to show with Susan. She already doesn't behave normally for a kid of her age. She spends half her time spying on the neighbours. Let's face it, that's sad."

"She what?"

"She spies on the neighbours. I've seen her. I suppose it's no worse than hanging around on street corners with a load of other ragamuffins, but it's not right all the same."

"Well it's her own fault. She ought to find something constructive to do."

"She doesn't know how to, you daft cow, you've never shown her."

"She's got friends to show her."

"She hasn't. You never stay in one place for long enough for her to make friends. You don't set her an example either, because you don't do that much that's constructive yourself."

"Well if that's what you think of me I don't know why you bother."

"I bother because I love you. I love you both."

"I don't get it. You've just told me I'm not constructive."

"That's because you didn't have anyone to show you how either. You spend your time painting your face and nails, watching soaps, shopping for clothes and going to the pub. But there are other things to do."

"Oh, shut up Shane, stop being so preachy, you're getting on my nerves. Get me another drink."

"No. Think of the baby."

"Bugger the baby. You can't expect me to run my whole life round it."

"Well actually that's pretty much what I do expect."

Imogen banged her empty glass down on the table and stormed out of the pub.

Chapter 20

Mikey loved the riffs. He blew a long note here and a group of two or three shorter ones there while Amos demonstrated his clarinettist's virtuosity. From under her thick blonde hair Ellen, transfixed, gazed with her big blue eyes at Amos's glistening face then watched the dancers, fascinated by the movement of foot and body, made difficult by the unpredictability of the music. Some did not even attempt to keep time but just seemed to enjoy shuffling around in the company of their partner. Others were able to create a pattern of movement that blended perfectly with the music for a few bars, only to lose the beat again a minute or two later. With cunningly intuitive footwork the most skilful were able to adjust to an unexpectedly long note or different cadence in a split second, and render an almost seamless performance. It was difficult to tear her eyes away from these.

As Ellen and her friends sat listening and watching, others were watching them. Among these were Mikey and Amos as well as a couple of relative newcomers to the Dugout. That is to say, Alan had been coming for about a year and a half now, whenever he could get the money together – usually as a result of winning the pot at Blues, for he was the most promising of all the players, but this was only Joe's second visit. Having now seen Ellen for himself Joe could understand why Alan had fallen for her, but he thought that making contact could be a delicate operation. However he was underestimating Alan' single mindedness.

"Look at that," said Amos, pointing during the second break. Sipping at his coke Mikey looked across to where Alan and Joe had joined Ellen and her friends and were now sitting at their table, chatting and animated.

Mikey couldn't believe his luck – or rather, Joe's luck, when he had seen Alan and Joe sidle up to the group and start a conversation.

"Early days."

"Well at least they've managed to introduce themselves. They're in."

"Yep." There was no doubt that Mikey was delighted beneath his low key response. Even if the whole thing petered out at least Joe was socialising with people of his own age and of both sexes. The snooker gang had its limitations. Some hours later, as the last stragglers were leaving, Ellen, her friend Becky, Joe and Alan were arranging a snooker challenge match for the following evening.

Chapter 21

"River Street, please."

Sheila sat back in the taxi and tried to subdue the butterflies in her stomach. She was more nervous than she had been the first time she had made this journey a few weeks ago. Then, nerves were unable to surface through the heady mixture of novelty, curiosity, excitement and sense of unreality that characterised that first brief encounter. Now, though, she and Simon having discovered that they wanted to see more of each other, and having resolved to meet again soon, for longer, Sheila had a sudden fear that they wouldn't like each other as much as they used to once they got to know each other properly again, having developed independently of each other over such a long period of time. She suspected that the conversation would be much more serious, probing, revealing. Her anxiety was being fed by the knowledge of the disapproval she would have to endure from their parents once it came out, as she knew it would, that she and Simon were back in touch with each other.

Meanwhile Simon, back in the cottage which was just as tumbledown, if not more so, as it had been when he had first moved in, was having the same feelings. Maybe it was worse for him, since he was, as it were, the sinner and therefore, unlike Sheila, in need of forgiveness.

"How did it go at Oxford? You never told me."

"They pushed me through with a third. I didn't do much work."

"Oh Simon! You could easily got a first."

"It doesn't really matter unless I suddenly decide I want to do further academic work, which I don't, and when you go for a job, which I'm not thinking of doing at the moment, people rarely ask you what class of degree you got. My heart wasn't in it really. I don't know why. I had so been looking forward to going to Oxford in the first place, but for some reason by the time I got there history seemed terribly unimportant."

"Do you think it had anything to do with what happened – you know, just before you left home?"

They looked at each other. Simon said hesitantly,

"What did they tell you?" and Sheila recounted the whole thing from Denise's point of view, saying finally,

"... and the whole thing would have been hilariously funny if the consequences hadn't been so extreme. Denise certainly thought it was, but of course she had no idea of the way it affected the rest of us."

Simon smile wryly.

"I can see what you mean. It'll never be funny for me, though. I've been through hell. I felt like some beastly animal and it changed my life. And let's face it, it was lucky that it was Denise who caught it, what with her approach to things and her general attitude – obviously it was water to a duck's back. But I didn't know that. And had it been, well, someone without such a raunchy personality I could have put them off men for life."

"Well, it wasn't, and it hasn't," said Sheila firmly and brightly, afraid that he was going to cry, and also rather subdued by the way he put it. In her relief at the way that Denise had described it she had decided that it had all been a storm in a teacup, but now Simon was making her see a more serious side to it. Her brother sexually out of control – wasn't that what happened with rapists? But surely this was exaggeration. Something of the sort had happened to her a couple of times, albeit in situations where drinking had been involved. She hadn't liked it and it had made her more wary, but she had got over it quickly enough. And Simon hadn't deliberately initiated the situation with Denise – she had unintentionally fallen against him. Sheila thought that perhaps they should move on, put the whole thing down to youth and lack of experience as well to the times they lived in. She felt considerable compassion for Simon, who was clearly still afflicted with at least the remnants of guilt and self-disgust.

"It's a shame if it affected your studies, but at least you've got a degree."

"Quite. I can always fall back on it if the painting comes to nothing. And it may come to nothing. I feel that I have aptitude, but actual talent, I don't know."

"What made you start in the first place?"

"I think it's to do with the way I've felt since I left home, or maybe even before I left home. It's about feelings, identity, connections, that kind of thing. Something was missing, and I thought painting might supply that thing."

He fell silent, correctly doubting Sheila's understanding of such things and not wanting to bore or patronise. She was very competent in the area of her own interests which were more securely attached than his to the physical world. And however could she ever understand about his fear of girls? She had known that they had pursued him relentlessly, but he could never make anyone understand how terrifying that had been.

"Have you had many girlfriends?" She laughed. "You may have one now, for all I know, I forgot to ask you, being foot loose and fancy free myself."

Simon disengaged his eyes from hers and looked at the floor.

"No."

Sheila had a sudden thought, "Simon, you're not *gay*, are you? It didn't sound as though you were when you were kissing Denise."

He looked at her intently. "I don't know. I don't think so, but I've never actually had a girlfriend."

"Have you had a boyfriend?"

"Sort of."

"Is it still going on?"

"Good question. I hope not but I'm not sure. The trouble is, I quite like the guy, but I'd been using him. When I realised this I eventually tried to escape, but he's very tenacious. At this moment I'm not sure whether he's given up or not. Do you remember those phone calls that you took when you were here before, when the caller hung up without saying anything? I'm pretty sure that was him. There was never anything physical between us, I really couldn't face it, so I suppose I'm not gay, but I haven't been able to connect with women, they terrify me, so I suppose he was some kind of 'emotional substitute' as they say, unless I'm bisexual or asexual, who knows?"

"So, what now?"

"How d' you mean? With the painting I'll persevere for a while, though it'll be harder without Quentin's financial input. I suppose I'll just have to stand firm. If I'm honest I can see that the lure of his money will make me cave in if I'm not careful. I want to keep painting and I hate poverty. That may be my choice at the moment – painting and Quentin, or, say, teaching and independence. Also, just to make everything more complicated, I think I've got a kind of Gauguin phase coming on, although I feel more inclined to go to the Caribbean than the South Pacific. Of course the Caribbean mightn't be remote enough to give me the effect I want. It's about the intensity of colour that I would expect to find there, and a totally different culture obviously, but unless I can sell more work it'll never happen without Quentin's money."

"That sounds so exciting, but I'd miss you and I've only just found you again. I'd love to come with you, though I'm not sure that I could afford the time or the money either. I've just signed up for a course in interior design."

"Really? You're probably doing the right thing. You were already quite interested in that a long time ago, before you opened your riding stables. What about riding though? You used to be terrifically keen."

"Since we last met the orthopaedic surgeon has advised me to find something else to do. My back problems from the accident I told you about are unlikely to heal fully. Also, I haven't properly recovered my nerve. It has been a bit of an emotional wrench I admit, but I've decided to take his advice, and I really do want to do interior design which, unlike horse-riding, I can continue with indefinitely. I can always have a sedate ride on one of Rachit and Natasha's horses if I want – I still see a lot of them, and they still offer me a fabulous social life, bless them, when I want it. You do remember Natasha, I presume?"

"Little Natasha Singh?"

"The very same. Not so little now, though. She's off to university in the autumn."

"Oxford?"

Sheila laughed.

"Not if she can help it. What kind of social life do you have yourself?"

Simon got up and refilled the kettle.

"I don't, really. I have to eat like everyone else, so I talk to people a bit in the village shop. It doesn't sell socks or paint brushes, though, so for that I get the bus to Sherborne and get to talk to the driver for a minute or two, or even another passenger. Once in town the opportunities are endless. I may talk to people in the library, or in Waterstones if I sit with a book on one of their comfortable sofas. At one of the supermarkets I stock up on food and other necessities and have a chat with the person on the checkout. They are usually quite happy to keep the queue waiting for a couple of minutes. Until three years ago I had

Quentin, and I really had to steel myself to bawl him out – I knew it would be grim without him, the loneliness as well as the poverty, but I suppose like lots of other artists I live in the belief that one day I will make it, if not the big time then at least enough to live decently – after all, some people manage to. Then I might find myself in a position to socialise a bit. Before that I had a really good friend living in this actual village – Kate – she wasn't a girlfriend, she was married, and funnily enough had known Quentin since they were children. It was because they met again through me that they renewed their friendship. She and I kept in touch after they left the village because of her husband's job, but that lapsed when I decided I had to get rid of Quentin."

"No parties then? No dinner dates?"

"Nope. Nothing. Although funnily enough I've just had a letter from Kate inviting me to a street party in honour of the Queen's Golden Jubilee. I sort of want to go – I'd love to see her and the kids again. The trouble is, Quentin will be there. Kate reckons he's over me and won't give me any grief, but I'm not too sure. I think he may have a secret agenda that she doesn't know about. And if he's 'friendly but distant', so to speak, maybe I won't be able to handle it myself. I'm feeling a bit fragile, and to have it confirmed that my one time friend and patron is permanently out of my life is going to make me feel appallingly vulnerable, even though it has been my own choice."

Simon brought Sheila a fresh cup of tea. She stirred it thoughtfully. As children she had always been Simon's protector in certain ways, even though he was the elder, and again she felt that sense of protectiveness rising within her.

"Perhaps we could go together," she suggested. "It might make you feel a bit safer. It would be a real shame if circumstances forced you into never seeing your friends again, especially as you have so few."

That's a bit patronising, she thought, so she said,

"And now that we're renegotiating our own relationship it may help us to catch up some of the time we've lost."

Simon stared. "Would you really?"

"Of course. Incidentally, from a combination of what you've said and the things Natasha's been telling me recently, I suspect that by some bizarre coincidence your friend Kate and Natasha's step-aunt Kate may be one and the same person. If I'm right Natasha could be there too. What do you think of that?"

"You're kidding!"

"No. It's true."

"Wow! I'd love to see her again!"

Chapter 22

"Get the door could you Quentin."

Kate hoped that Quentin would hear, given that she was in the bath with a face pack on. It was one of those that went hard, so it was difficult to shout distinctly.

Quentin put down his newspaper and got up out of David's favourite armchair. David wasn't home yet. Quentin knew, more or less, what Kate was doing upstairs and couldn't help wondering what all the fuss was about and why Kate felt the need to do herself up like a dog's dinner for this particular guest. He went to the front door, opened it and stared, rather rudely as it happens, for several seconds.

"Hi," said the apparition. "I'm Natasha. I hope I've come to the right house."

"Oh...yes," said Quentin, overwhelmed by a feeling of déjà vu. He hadn't experienced this sensation since the time he first came face to face with Simon, over ten years ago. Natasha was a knockout.

Kate, meanwhile, hearing the voices below, realised that Natasha had arrived and thanked her lucky stars that it was Quentin and not the children who had answered the door. Quentin was charm personified in these situations, even when he didn't particularly like the person he had just met. His reliability in such matters, his impeccable manners and natural courtesy, were some of the things about him that enchanted Kate the most. She couldn't help but forgive him therefore when, discovering on occasion that he didn't like the new acquaintance, he retreated into an abstruse irony, usually so subtle that the victim failed to detect it.

Kate wasn't ready firstly because no one had known at precisely what time Natasha was likely to arrive, and secondly because of all those childhood memories of living in the same family as Daphne, Natasha's snooty mother. Kate had always been made to feel badly dressed, gauche and generally inadequate. She was determined that Natasha would have nothing adverse about the Dawson household in general and Kate herself in particular to report back to her mother. As a result Kate had spent the best part of the day planning the meals for the entire duration of Natasha's short stay and preparing that evening's meal. Luckily she was so focused on food at the moment because of the impending street party that none of this was as difficult as it otherwise might have been. In the freezer, the fridge and the kitchen in general she had pretty much every kind of foodstuff that the planet had to offer. That evening's meal planned and prepared to perfection, Kate had nothing to worry about now except giving herself an appearance to match.

From her own room Kate heard Quentin show Natasha up to hers. She heard Natasha's footsteps going back downstairs a few minutes after Quentin's. Kate hoped that she herself wouldn't get a black mark for not being down in time to welcome her on arrival.

She needn't have worried. By the time she got downstairs there was a veritable party atmosphere, with Natasha, Quentin and the twins chattering and laughing merrily. It was as though Natasha had arrived with a pocketful of feel-good dust and had sprinkled it through the house. Kate immediately felt cheerful herself.

Quentin turned as she entered and stared for a second time. He couldn't quite believe that the person standing in front of him was Kate. She looked terrific, and the elegant way in which Quentin poured and presented her with a glass of red wine made Kate feel like a million dollars.

It was clear to Kate that Quentin was feeling a great deal better than he had two or three weeks ago. Then, he had been nervy and agitated, had burst into tears a couple of times and come home from a short trip to London looking distinctly jaded. This had been very worrying, because not only was Kate afraid that he would become ill again, but also that she might have done the wrong thing in writing to Simon and inviting him to the street party. She had only done so with the best intentions. She had of course consulted Quentin, and he had seemed quite relaxed about it. He had just had another couple of days in London and thankfully was beginning to perk up, and now he was flirting with Natasha, who was loving it. This was delightful and threatening at the same time. When Quentin was down, although Kate hated to see him unhappy she felt safe, that he needed her and that he wouldn't run off taking his eccentric companionability with him, leaving her with a dull, tense marriage to cope with on her own. She wanted him well and happy, but she didn't want him to leave, a thing that he easily might do – after all he had that lovely house in Oxfordshire, on which he had spent so much time and money, to go and live in. She could imagine the wonderful life he would have – literary evenings, cocktail parties, barbecues, fascinating conversation and a burgeoning career, and now, realising he could genuinely command the attention of a fabulous young woman like Natasha simply by being himself, his self-confidence was visibly growing. And although Kate knew this confidence could evaporate just as quickly as it had arrived she felt a pang of jealously to realise that although Quentin would always be heavily dependent on someone it wouldn't always be her, Kate.

However Kate wasn't quite as frightened of Quentin leaving as she had been. This was because in the last few days she had seen a ray of hope for her marriage. It wasn't much, but it was something. David had been far less grouchy since about a fortnight ago, when she had been surprised at some of his concessions over the street party arrangements. She thought this was partly because he had got his way in respect of the time and place of the royal celebration, and another factor was perhaps that he had been preoccupied at work – the Friday evening meetings in particular, which had been suddenly terminated, had seemed to be taking up a lot of his time. On Friday last week, though, he had come home much earlier than usual – the twins hadn't even gone to bed, though admittedly they stayed up later than usual on Fridays. Instead of going straight to his study or retreating behind the newspaper David had smiled when he came in, given her a hug and offered to make everyone a hot drink. She had been truly surprised. Since then he had been pleasanter than usual – just in little ways it's true, but it had been very noticeable.

"Really, Kate, are you going to speak to our guest or not?" enquired Quentin amiably. "You've been standing there for five minutes at least without saying a word."

"A chance would be a fine thing," retorted Kate who, although guilty of having slipped quite unintentionally into a reverie, had nevertheless been semi-aware of the non-stop chatter. She began to make polite enquiries about Natasha's plans, her mother and so forth when David came in, bright and breezy.

"Evening, all," he called from the hall. He came through to the lounge, kissed the twins, said "Evening, Quentin," and gave Kate a hug. Then he turned towards Natasha and, like the others, did a double take. Catching his breath he said, "You must be Natasha. Lovely to meet you."

Natasha wasn't at all surprised by anything that was going on. She hadn't had any particular expectations. She was enjoying herself. It was interesting and fun to be meeting these relatives of whom she'd heard tell. She was finding, as expected, that her mother had been talking nonsense. They were all so nice, especially Quentin, but she liked the others too. She was not remotely thrown by Kate's glamorous appearance – newly made-up and generally immaculate at the end of what, presumably, had already been a long day. This would have been absolutely normal for her own mother. She was not surprised either that Kate was not only not frumpy and dull but, rather, highly intelligent and articulate. But Natasha, faultlessly groomed socially by her parents, was calm and confident in every conceivable situation.

As for Quentin he was quite inebriated on the success he was having with Natasha. If anyone had mentioned Simon at this point he would have looked puzzled, for at this moment Quentin had actually forgotten who Simon was. When he finally recognised this fact for himself he had a strange rush of feeling in control of his life at last, a feeling which had been absent for so many years that the contrast made him feel quite giddy. At this moment Quentin was totally light-headed and couldn't have cared less whether or not he ever saw or heard of Simon again.

"Will you be joining us for our Golden Jubilee street party?" he implored, rather than enquired of, Natasha.

"I'd love to. I've got no exams at all that week. It's a late half term for us, simply because of the timing of the Jubilee."

"Right-o. I'll just go and let Kate know now. Then you'll be sure of a room here. There's no knowing who else she might be planning to invite."

Chapter 23

It was the second Saturday in May and Susan was fed up. She would rather have been at school. She liked the feeling of having lots of people around her. She hadn't really got any friends yet – the other kids were wary of her hostile demeanour, born of loneliness and insecurity, and in any case she hadn't been there long. As she walked along the school corridors at change of lessons she always looked out for Jack and Chloe, even though she knew that they would both turn their gaze away from her as they passed – he from embarrassment, she with disdain. The actual interaction between the three of them had been scanty, but the general antipathy emanating from the twins was unmistakable. Susan, incorrectly, felt sure that Jack must have told Chloe about what had happened. If only she hadn't done it. They would never want to be friends with her now.

Now, however, there was little for Susan to do. She had no money with which to entertain herself. Yesterday a row with her mother for not allowing her to try and get a paper round on account of the fact that she was under age had caused Susan to stamp her foot and shout back in frustration.

"Don't get hormonal with me, young lady," Imogen had said. She shared with Kathleen the belief that hormones were to blame for more things than most people gave them credit for. But Susan had nowhere to channel the restless energy that was welling up inside her.

Right now Shane was tinkering with his car and Imogen was still in bed, fuelling the resentment that Susan felt against her mother, a resentment accompanied by the anxiety that Shane and Imogen hadn't been getting on too well of late, and Susan was afraid that maybe they were going to split up. She was desperate for them to stay together. Shane was the first of Imogen's boyfriends whom Susan had really liked. He was the first to take a serious personal interest in her. He had taken her to the fair on Monday afternoon, a rare treat, while Imogen went to get her hair coloured. It had been fantastic, but today he had told her firmly that she would have to find herself something to do as her mother was feeling sick and he had the car to fix.

She tiptoed to the window. The street seemed deserted. The glorious weather had been forecast some days in advance and lots of people were away for the day or for the weekend. She looked up the street to her right, where Joe and Mikey's house was, two up from The Grange, but nothing stirred. Mikey, as it happened, had gone round to Amos's house for a music practice, being unable to do it at home at the moment on account of the quiet Joe needed to revise for his exams. Joe normally studied in the library when he wasn't at school, but it was becoming very crowded on Saturdays with so many children revising, and he couldn't always find somewhere convenient to sit. The Grange opposite had the same air of abandonment.

Susan looked down the street to her left, and saw Sid digging in his garden. She went and listened outside her mother's door for signs of life. Imogen stirred, then settled down again with a sigh. I think she's almost awake, thought Susan. She went to the bathroom and closed the door quietly. She waited for a couple of moments then flushed the toilet. She was hoping the sound of the flush and then the cistern refilling would be enough to cover the sound of her opening and closing the front door without being enough to wake Imogen completely. She would worry about the consequences of going out without permission when she got back.

Sid let her stand on the pavement, looking over the fence for a while before he spoke. Being such a mild, gentle-mannered man he didn't want to intrude – wanting something to watch and wanting someone to talk to were two different things. Eventually he said,

"Want a glass of lemonade?"

"Yes, please."

"I suppose you're another one with nothing to do, then?"

"Another what?"

Sid laughed. "That would be telling. Seems to me that youngsters today got no ideal of how to fill their spare time. At your age I'd have been off on me bike with me mates, into the countryside with an apple in me pocket, looking for streams to dam and trees to climb."

"What for?"

Sid stared at her. "For the joy o' living of course."

"I wouldn't want to do that. Anyway, I don't think I would be allowed to."

"Course you would. You'd be quite safe if you went with some friends."

"I haven't got any friends."

"Well, I suppose you haven't been here long enough, have you? What about those Dawson kids?"

"They don't like me."

"How d' you know? Told you that, did they?"

"No."

"You need to be a bit bold."

"What do you mean?"

"Well now, there's two of them, isn't there, and they've got their friends already, seeing as they've been here four or five years. The little lass goes dancing too, talented I believe,

151

though I'm not sure as the lad has much to occupy him other than a bit of football now and then. But you need them more than they need you, so it's up to you to make the first move."

Susan felt hot all over as she remembered what she had done a couple of weeks back.

"I sort of did. I can't. I did something stupid. They'll never like me now."

"What did you do?"

"I can't tell you."

Sid sat and thought for a minute. Storm in a tea cup I dare say, he thought. Bit of a neglected kid she is though, probably stuck her tongue out, showed her thrupennies, sommat like that, I shouldn't wonder.

"The thing is, you gotta persevere."

"Persevere?"

"Yes. Keep at it. Don't give up. Keep being nice to them."

"How?"

"Anything. Smile at them. After a few times give a little wave, even if they haven't smiled back. If they pass close enough to hear, say hello. Don't give up. Keep doing it till one of them smiles back. It'll work in the end if you don't give up."

"It'll never happen."

"Not true. Have you ever really tried hard at something?"

"Um ... I don't remember."

Susan was beginning to take heart. No one had ever talked to her like this before, not even Shane. It was as though Sid actually understood how she was feeling and the problems she was having. She was sure he was mistaken – but maybe he wasn't. Grown-ups did get it right sometimes. This thought made her feel much better, much braver.

She looked up and across to the window of the flat where she lived and saw the curtains twitch. I'm for it now, she thought.

"Can I come and talk to you again?"

"Of course you can, my love. Of course you can."

Chapter 24

"Hurry up, Chloe, you're going to be late!"

I'd like a pound for every time I've said that, thought Kate, putting bread in the toaster and cornflakes on the table. But at least she only had Chloe to worry about on a Saturday morning – David, Jack and Quentin didn't normally get up until she and Chloe had left the house. And at least she no longer had to stay with Chloe during her Saturday morning lesson. This morning Kate had a lot to do between dropping Chloe off and picking her up again.

Chloe appeared sleepily at the door. Kate automatically picked up the hairbrush she kept next to the cooker and started to brush her daughter's hair.

"This needs cutting."

"*No,* Mum. I told you, I'm going to grow it as long as Little Clara's."

Kate sighed. Chloe had done nothing but eat and sleep Little Clara since last week's performance of The Nutcracker.

"Quentin sounds happy this morning," said Chloe.

"Oh?"

"Mm. He's whistling and singing and talking to the cat."

"*Most* odd," said Kate. And it was. Cheerfulness was not something one could normally accuse Quentin of. Witty and loud at times, yes. And of course he was frequently morose, withdrawn, petulant or querulous. It was true that Kate had begun to notice that the London trips seemed to improve Quentin's mood, then Natasha came last week and cast a spell over them all, and Quentin had been so chirpy for the next couple of days that if Kate hadn't known better she would have sworn that he had fallen in love with Natasha. Briefly, all his old charisma had returned. Until now he hadn't been this cheerful in Kate's presence since they had rediscovered each other in Dorset six or seven years ago. The euphoria created among them by Natasha's visit still clung in places, and another London visit since then and from which he had returned yesterday (the paper was very nearly ready now) seemed to have helped maintain his buoyant mood. Kate still hadn't got used to the new, almost bouncy Quentin, nor did she really believe it would last. For years he had been alternately manic and driven, whilst trying to direct and control his fated relationship with Simon, and tense and depressed when he appeared not to have been succeeding in this venture. He had seesawed between hyperactivity and inertia. There had been, of course, his two 'breakdowns', for want of a better word, one after the other, although maybe it had all been the same one, there was no telling.

"Maybe he had a really good time in London," said Chloe, "and it's cheered him up. Ursula's nice, isn't she? They ought to go out with each other."

Kate winced. There it was again, that jarring feeling – Chloe talking about relationships this time – a reminder that her two adorable little tots had become 'pre-teenagers'. The idyllic years of picnics and bedtime stories, the pleasures of which had far outweighed the disadvantages of childhood illnesses and the need for babysitters, were coming to an end. Kate was feeling this as quite a wrench, and sometimes found herself wondering whether she was still young enough to have another baby (or two) and whether or not David would stand for it, until she did the sums and a bit of mental projection and dismissed the idea. She was not anticipating the adolescent years with relish, but she was able to look forward to the time beyond that when they would enjoy all being adults together, and she would have a bit of time and space for herself.

Chloe hadn't been exaggerating. When David, an hour or so later, shuffled down to the kitchen for breakfast Quentin was already there, bright and breezy, still whistling (to David's slight irritation), wiping down the floral PVC tablecloth, loading the dishwasher and rearranging on the kitchen table the items that would be required by David for his breakfast. Quentin had had his own and given Jack his.

"Shall I make some tea?" asked Quentin brightly as David sat down at the table.

"If it's no trouble. Where's Jack?"

"I don't know. I think he went out."

"Damn. I hope he's back in time for the cricket."

"Cricket?"

"We're going to the County Ground after lunch."

"Didn't you go last week?"

"Yes. We enjoyed it. We're going as often as possible."

David, though pleased that it wasn't left to him, as it usually was on a Saturday morning, to clear up after Chloe and Kate and provide the rest of them with a fairly civilised breakfast environment, was somewhat put out by Quentin's buoyant mood. He could not remember ever having seen Quentin so thoroughly happy and pleasant, and didn't particularly want to now. Like Kate, he vaguely registered that this wasn't quite the first day that Quentin had been like this, though he wasn't absolutely sure when it had started. He had determined to be Mr Nice Guy himself, and although he could see that being nice to Quentin, which had to be part of this, was going to be much easier if Quentin himself was going to be nice, it would also make it harder for David to out-nice him, so to speak.

And oust Quentin he must, because David was horribly aware of the danger of his dalliance with Tracy developing into a full-blown affair, even though he didn't find her all that attractive. Her lure (as opposed to *al*lure), was triggered by default, a substitute with which he was compensating for the shortcomings in his marriage. Two weeks ago he had come home straight after the late meeting, at which he had announced to the assembled company that it would be the last. He suspected that although Kate in general didn't quit easily she was nevertheless sufficiently disenchanted with their marriage to let him go if he chose to. David thought that their problems were at least half her fault, but he had come to realise that if he really wanted changes he would have to be the one to instigate them and not wait for her to do it, no matter whose fault the problems were.

Once it had crossed his mind, the idea of being without his family was unbearable. After all, what would he be left with? His work? He was disillusioned with his job at the moment. True, he and his team did make a significant difference in the lives of a few families and individuals, and a temporary or less significant improvement for some others. But in many, many cases the involvement of the social services in people's lives was, he suspected, not nearly as effective as they claimed it to be, and in some cases did more harm than good. Yet that made it worth doing, surely, if only for the few? But this wasn't what he wanted. This wasn't what he had joined up for. He had had a vision, a belief that he had a crusade to lead and that under its banner the enemy – poverty, ignorance, inequality, crime and ill-health, would be overcome. He felt like laughing at the egoism of the young man he once had been. He could now see that career wise he had two choices – to accept the limitations of social work and carry on regardless or put his energies into something else.

As David started on his second piece of toast he was surprised to notice that Quentin was still in the kitchen – and heavens, what was he doing? Peeling potatoes! It was impossible for David to let such a thing pass without comment.

"Earning your keep, then," he remarked.

Got that wrong, he thought. So much for being nice.

"Yes, well of course Kate's always in a rush when she comes back with Chloe from dancing. I thought maybe I should give her a hand – I probably don't do enough to help, one way and another."

David couldn't think of a suitable reply to this without being patronising, unkind or incriminating himself, so he said,

"How important do you think it is to make a worthwhile contribution to the world, Quentin?"

Now it was Quentin's turn to be surprised.

"I'm not sure. Why do you ask?"

"I'm fed up with my job. I'm beginning to wonder if there's any point in carrying on, or even whether I'm doing any good."

"Good grief. This is awfully deep for breakfast time."

"I suppose it is. I think maybe it's been building up."

"People don't agree about what is or isn't worthwhile, for a start. Maybe everything is, maybe everything which isn't actually wrong or harmful is worth doing, not only for any beneficial results, but merely for the doing of it, if you see what I mean. I think what you have to do is find out who you are and be it. Everything else will follow of its own accord."

David recognised one of the things about Quentin which really annoyed him. He sometimes talked such a load of rubbish.

"Thanks, Quentin," he said, getting up and brushing the crumbs from the front of his shirt. "I'll see you later."

The main reason for Quentin's elated mood, although he wouldn't have been willing to acknowledge it, was the fact that the day of the street party was getting nearer and he had every hope that Simon would be there. He knew of course that Kate had invited him, and Natasha's influence over his state of mind was fading in her absence, allowing the old habit of feeling to partly re-emerge. However after his sensible conversation with Ursula the day before yesterday (he was seeing her – professionally – twice a week at the moment) he was pleased and surprised to find that he really did feel that he could be just ordinary friends with Simon and nothing more. The appearance of the delectable Natasha had helped with this. It wasn't exactly that he saw her as a second string to his bow – after all, she was hardly going to become his girlfriend, particularly in view of the age difference. But there was something about her that made her seriously worthy of his interest, simply as a fellow human being, *and she might be coming to Bristol for the next four years.* Natasha was the most beautiful woman he had ever seen - bar his mother, which wasn't the same thing - just as Simon was the most beautiful man he had ever seen bar none. Like Simon she was bright. Unlike Simon she was also confident, witty, refined and communicated clearly. And she was oh, so nice! Quentin saw the possibility of being able to adore her. And adoration would be so much less complicated than an actual relationship. It struck him for the first time that it could have been adoration, not love, that he had felt for Simon, but if so the adoration had been annihilated by the exhaustion of the relationship, and if adoration without desire for possession could be provided by Natasha then maybe this was his best bet. What had occurred to him during his long chat over dinner with Ursula was that there would be a *permanence,* however faint, about his relationship with Simon if he let go now without annoying or alarming him further, and this would be in addition to the historical permanence of what they had been to each other in years gone by, which could never be changed. Nothing could un-happen it, but its memory could be damaged if he continued to behave in an irrational way.

Quentin was moving on.

Chapter 25

Dainty's brow was furrowed with the effort of so much writing. She and Kate were embarked on yet another street party list. After a while she put down the pencil to pick up the mug of coffee Kate had put at her elbow. She sipped the coffee and watched Kate rustling through a recipe book of desserts, humming as she did so. The change in Kate's habitual facial expression was so marked that eventually Dainty succumbed to the desire to comment. Gone were the lines of tension, and could that be a little smile playing round the corners of her mouth?

"You the cat that got the cream?"

"I beg your pardon?"

"You look happy."

It took Kate a moment or two to absorb this idea. The comment seemed rather personal, intrusive. She felt ruffled for a moment, then realised that actually she did have a feeling of contentment for the first time since she couldn't remember when.

"Do I?"

"Yeah. Has something happened?"

It had and it hadn't. Kate had spent so long never telling anyone how she felt that she was no longer aware of actually feeling anything other than general anxiety and resentment. Now put on the spot by Dainty she realised that although she didn't seem to feel anything in particular at the moment this in itself was a novelty and a plus. It meant that for once neither resentment nor anxiety was present.

"Well, yes and no."

Dainty cupped her chin in her hands. "Please elaborate."

Kate hesitated. "Well ... I think it's David."

"Yes?" Dainty's black eyes were fixed, unwavering, on Kate's face.

"Well, he's being incredibly nice."

"Isn't he always?"

"Well ... no. Or at least, I don't think so."

"When did this change take place?"

"I think it started about three weeks ago." Kate felt as though she was in a trance. It was totally against her personality to be giving away such *personal* secrets, yet she herself was curious to discover the answers to Dainty's questions.

"What prompted this new behaviour?"

"I really have absolutely no idea. We haven't been getting on for absolutely ages. I don't really know why. One minute we were madly in love, getting on really well, getting married and divinely happy, then a few years down the line we were suddenly aware, or at least *I* was suddenly aware, that we weren't in love, that we bored each other, that we didn't like each other, that we resented each other even. Oh, Dainty, whatever went wrong?"

Kate burst into tears. She continued to sob for several minutes before it subsided. Dainty said,

"That's just the tension coming out. There's nothing to really cry about now, is there, if it's been sorted out."

Calming down, Kate dried her eyes.

"Isn't there? I don't know if anything *has* been sorted out. We haven't had a conversation about it or anything, it's just that he says hello when he comes in instead of ignoring me, asks what kind of day I've had, how the twins are – he's even brought me flowers a couple of times. I haven't been doing anything different, so I don't know why he's decided to be like this."

"You don't need to know now, you'll find out later, but if you want it to stay like this you'll have to encourage him."

"I've just started thinking about that. The trouble is, it's really difficult. I have to force myself to smile and speak to him in a friendly way. I'm just not used to it, I've felt so alienated from him for years. It's such hard work that sometimes I think I'd like to go back to how it was."

"Do you want to keep your marriage or not?"

"Yes."

"But you don't want to make the effort to make it work. Why's that? Is it because you're sure that he's been wrong and you've been right about every issue you've had in the past? And that he will never learn? Is it because you need him to be perfect in every way and agree with your views at all times before you will begin to forgive him for the times he did get it wrong, before you will look at the mistakes you might have made and make an effort yourself? Even though he is making an effort? If that's the case you gonna be a lonely lady. If that's the case you'll always be alone, because there ain't no man in the world will be good enough for you."

Kate was speechless. What Dainty lacked in literacy she certainly compensated for with her rhetorical acumen. Dainty had put her finger on it, and now Kate felt really small.

"You're right, Dainty. I feel really small."

Dainty slapped her thigh and roared with laughter.

"Small you ain't, sweetheart. You're a big-hearted girl, but I see the stubbornness in you, same as my sister. She knows full well who is the father of her baby, and I have my suspicions of my own. If he's who I think he is then handsome he ain't, but he's got a kind heart and would make her a good husband, but she wants her freedom and he wants a church wedding, so she says, and she won't have nuttin' to do with him. Personally I think she's twisting the truth. I think it's his brother Piety wants. Now there's a good-looking guy, you better believe it. But if she's hanging on for him she gonna be disappointed."

"Well, if the ugly one knows he's the father of the baby he could fight it."

"We'll see, we'll see. Where we come from folks sort out things among themselves, we don't go axin' permission from no judge, but we'll see."

Chapter 26

It was nearly two o'clock when Kate, Chloe and Naomi came through the back door and into the kitchen.

"Gracious!" said Kate. "Someone's peeled the potatoes again!"

Chloe dropped her shoe bag onto the floor.

"Must have been the same fairy as last week," she said. It was a minor mystery – no one had owned up to it and they couldn't imagine either David or Quentin having done it, let alone Jack.

There was a cough from the doorway into the hall, and there stood Quentin holding out a bunch of flowers. "I'm not sure that I want to be referred to as a fairy," he said.

"Oh, Quentin, how lovely! Freesias! Are you trying to make David jealous?"

"Hardly. And speaking of David, something seems to have happened to him, have you noticed?"

"Like what?"

Quentin was about to say that David had been behaving like a normal human being for a change when he suddenly registered Chloe and Naomi's presence, and said instead:

"How's the ballet going, Chloe?"

"Fantastic!" said Kate.

"I can speak for myself, Mum."

"Sorry, darling."

The front doorbell rang. Kate went across the hall to open it and found Kathleen standing there with Imogen. Susan had come too.

"Work party," announced Kathleen, stepping across the threshold as though she was one of the family.

"Well hello! Come in! Put the kettle on would you, Kathleen. We're not quite ready, the girls and I have just got back from ballet. Go upstairs and get changed, girls, then come down for a sandwich."

Kate had been in too much of a hurry to wait for Chloe and Naomi to change immediately after their class. She led the newcomers into the largest kitchen Imogen had ever seen in a private house. As Chloe went through the hall with Naomi she directed towards Susan the filthiest look she could muster – a devastatingly withering stare that she and Jack had perfected over a number of years – but to no avail since Susan was looking the other way.

"That's *her*," Chloe hissed to Naomi, but by the time Naomi had woken up to what she meant the moment had passed and Susan had disappeared into the kitchen.

"Coffee?" Kathleen enquired of those assembled. She was pleased to be seen by Imogen and Susan as being treated with such relaxed familiarity in the Dawson house.

"Please," said Imogen.

"No thanks," said Kate.

Kathleen made the coffee and gave a mugful to Imogen and a glass of coke to Susan.

"I'm off then, love," she said, "I only came to introduce these two. I can't remember whether I told you that I can't stay more than a few minutes this morning. I'm helping Wendy get her stall ready for the church fete next Saturday."

"I'll see you at the street party meeting next week, then. Thanks for bringing them."

"I'll let m' self out," said Kathleen, and disappeared into the hall.

"Where's Jack?" enquired Susan.

"Susan!" said her mother.

"What's wrong?"

"Remember your manners. Don't be nosey."

Uptight relationship, thought Kate. She laughed.

"Jack's gone to watch the cricket with his father. Second match of the season, actually, at our county ground at least. Have you two had lunch?"

"Yes, Thanks."

"Well then give me your coats and things and make yourselves comfortable. I'll be ready in a minute."

She made some sandwiches for herself, Chloe and Naomi. The two girls came downstairs.

"Pooh, what a dreadful smell," said Chloe. Naomi giggled.

Kate sniffed the air. "I can't smell anything."

"It's a real pong," said Chloe, "like there's something really disgusting in here." Naomi's face was bright pink, and she was holding her lips tight and looking as though she might explode.

"Can you smell anything, Imogen?"

"No, and I don't think they can either." Imogen's pretty face was set, her expression sour. She was quick to detect hostility – far more so than the trained social worker facing her across the table – however covert it might be. As a life-long victim herself she was hyper-vigilant.

Sensing trouble Kate glared at Chloe, and quickly changing the subject she turned to Imogen.

"Kathleen said that you had offered to make something for the street party."

"Well, I don't really cook but I can make trifle."

"Trifle would be great. What do you eat at home if you don't cook?"

"Shane cooks. I sometimes do burgers and stuff, but nothing fancy."

"For heaven's sake, Mum, you can have a perfectly healthy diet without cooking anything. Cheese sandwiches and apples, for example." In recent weeks both Chloe and Naomi had taken to talking to their parents as though they were congenital idiots.

"Yeah, right," said Kate.

Lunch over, Kate said, "You three can either go and play upstairs or play outside, but don't get under our feet."

"I'd rather stay and help," said Susan quickly.

"You'll do as you're told," said Imogen.

"It's okay," said Kate, "an extra pair of hands always comes in useful. Those two seem to be going through a 'phase', so I can quite understand Susan treating them with caution, especially as she doesn't know them. They're a bit 'them and us' at the moment I'm ashamed to say, it's tribal I think, and probably something to do with their ballet as well, I'm sure it'll be fine when they all get to know each other a bit better. Are you beginning to make friends at school, Susan?"

"No."

"You soon will. I'm jolly glad of your help anyway."

Kate then gave three large lemons to Susan and a quantity of smoked mackerel to Imogen.

"Lemons halved and juiced in the juicer, smoked mackerel skinned and boned and put through the mixer. Tell me when you've finished and I'll tell you what to do next. I'm not quite sure that we'll need it all, what with all the other food we've got and all the things that other people are bringing on the day, so I'm going to freeze it in portions just in case. Are you settling in all right? I meant to ask you over as soon as I realised that you'd moved in, but you know how it is. I don't know where the time goes."

"We're fine. Shane's been helping us. He's local. We've got the flat straight now."

Quentin came back into the kitchen just then. "Hello, Susan," he said.

"Hello."

"I didn't know you two knew each other."

"Our little secret. We met in the newsagent's actually. Susan gave me to understand that she would like to be introduced to Flopsy and Cottontail someday."

"I'm surprised the twins haven't invited her over already," said Kate untruthfully.

"I'm not," said Quentin. "I don't think you realise how incestuous those two little buggers are, Kate. As long as they've got each other they wouldn't care if there was nobody else on the planet. You need to watch that you know. It's seriously anti-social."

"Don't be silly, Quentin. Twins are different, that's all it is. They'll grow out of it when they discover the opposite sex."

Quentin turned to Imogen and beamed.

"Well, well, a visit from our new neighbour at last. Are you going to introduce us, Kate? And do I smell coffee brewing? Delightful."

Quentin was on form again, as he increasingly was, and once again Kate experienced her feeling of bafflement as to how this hugely likeable man got his relationships into such a muddle.

"It may need warming up. This is Imogen. Imogen, Quentin. By the way, what were you going to say about

David?" She suspected she ought not to ask in front of the neighbours, but her curiosity got the better of her.

"Only how charmingly friendly he is these days."

We'll continue this later, thought Kate. David charmingly friendly and Quentin cheerful, whatever was the world coming to? But now that the pair of them were behaving so much better she was beginning to realise what a lot they had been taking out of her with their moodiness and irritability.

Quentin sat down at the kitchen table and continued to beam at Imogen, who was rapidly beginning to relax in the warmth emanating from Quentin like melting snow in the sunshine. Kate was amazed at the charm oozing out of him, and had a sudden flashback to the Quentin of fifteen and twenty years ago. She had quite forgotten that he could be like this. He had obviously taken an instant shine to Imogen in spite of her air of ignorance and lack of education, and she to him. Kate had seen this before with Quentin. It was both puzzling and delightful at the same time. He often turned his nose up at those who usually commanded at least some respect, David's colleagues for example, or even some of his own Oxford colleagues, on the grounds with the first group that they were as thick as pig shit and not worth a moment of his time or attention, with the second group that they were arrogant, idle and bigoted. Yet he adored Kathleen, Jack and Chloe and others whom she would not expect to interest him, whilst holding a distant respect for the likes of Sid and Mikey, with whom he hadn't so far found much common ground.

The afternoon wore on happily and busily. It seemed that Quentin had nothing particular to do that afternoon and he sat in the rocking chair by the kitchen window leafing through recipe books. This unprecedented behaviour seemed a mark of Quentin's new, mellow state of mind. Kate, who normally might have made an ironic comment about this, held her peace for fear of frightening him away. It was rather nice, somehow, having him sitting there browsing while the three of them busied themselves with street party fare. His effect on the newcomers was marvellous. They had become relaxed and animated, which removed from Kate's mind the fear of having nothing to talk about. Imogen and Susan prattled away and Kate was able to focus on what she was doing rather than on them. As a side benefit Susan made tea or coffee as required and in the meantime Kate got all kinds of snippets of information about their lives without having to ask and risk putting her foot in it, although a lot was clearly being withheld. Of course they would withhold it from a snobbish, bigoted middle class pair like you and Quentin, a little voice (David's) said in her head.

After a while Kate talked a bit about herself and the rest of the family, and her visitors seemed quite interested and often stopped her to ask a question. None of them noticed that the light drizzle which had begun just after

Susan and Imogen arrived had become a downpour and they were all, consequently, quite startled when David and Jack, soaking wet, burst in through the kitchen door.

"Good gracious!" exclaimed Kate.

"Rain stopped play," announced Jack, trying to dry his face with the sleeve of his dripping jacket. Susan blushed furiously, and bent her head over the apples she was slicing. Jack, suddenly realising who the visitors were, made a dash for the door into the hall.

"Where do you think you are going?" snapped Kate."

"Upstairs."

"Not in those wet things. Don't go a step further until you've taken off those shoes and that coat."

In desperation Jack fumbled at his clothing, feeling that something appalling would happen if he didn't succeed in getting out of the kitchen in the next few seconds. He kicked off his shoes, tore off his coat, dropped both on the floor and bolted upstairs. After a moment of indecision, due to the presence of visitors, Kate picked them up herself and deposited them in the adjacent laundry room.

Chloe opened the door of her bedroom and stood there haughtily.

"What's the rush?"

"Mind your own business."

Jack startled himself. He had never before spoken to Chloe in such a way, being so emotionally dependent on her and afraid of alienating her, and wasn't sure why he had done so now. The shock of the sight of Susan in his own house followed by Chloe's supercilious attitude might have had something to do with it. He went into his room and slammed the door. It was opened a minute later by Chloe and Naomi, who shut it behind them and stood with their backs to it.

"Did you speak to her?" demanded Chloe.

"Who?"

"You know who. The tart downstairs. I believe her name is Susan."

"Of course not. I don't even know her, do I?"

"We hope not," said Naomi.

When they had come in Jack had started by being a bit frightened. Intimidation was something Chloe practised a lot. But now he suddenly felt angry.

"What's it got to do with you?"

"Everything," said Chloe. "There is my reputation to consider. I can't have my brother going out with the local scrubber."

"I'VE NEVER EVEN SPOKEN TO HER," screamed Jack. "YOU'RE MAD!"

It was Chloe's turn to be startled. She had never seen Jack do that before. Naomi, however, stayed calm.

"Let's keep it that way, then," she said. "When Chloe is a famous dancer the social connections made by her family will be extremely important to her career. We know that the bitch follows you and spies on you and wants you for herself. Be careful. Come on, Chloe."

They turned and left. Jack was shaking. He opened his door again and listened. They were back in Chloe's room again with the door shut. He could hear them talking, just above the sound of Chloe's CD player belting out 'YMCA'. He heard his mother yell from downstairs: "Turn that DOWN!"

Back in the privacy of Chloe's room Naomi said, "That wasn't meant to happen. I thought we were going to have a go at her, not him."

"I know," said Chloe, "but it doesn't really matter. He needs to know that he's got to toe the line, and we can have a go at her later."

All the same, she felt uncomfortable. She and Jack had never had a row before and it felt horrid, even though she knew she had started it. Somehow it didn't feel that way. It felt as though it had started all by itself, and she was wishing it hadn't happened. She wanted to go running to Jack and say she was sorry, she meant to have a go at Susan, not at him, that it wasn't really about being a famous ballerina, it was about the fact that they were both growing up and that seemed to make things happen which neither of them had planned. She wanted to say that she loved him and that she really didn't mind if he wanted to have a girlfriend – after all she had her ballet and so he was entitled to have something of his own, but it would have to be someone very special because they, Chloe and Jack, were special, weren't they? She wanted to tell him that she didn't need him to do as he was told any more, she didn't need someone to boss around now that she had her dancing. She wanted, in fact desperately needed him to understand how she was feeling, that she didn't want to separate from him but it was happening anyway, that deep down he was more to her than was Naomi, her best friend. Naomi might be Chloe's best friend (for the moment at least) but Jack was her twin brother and that meant that they were bound together forever in a very special way. However Chloe had her end to keep up so she said to Naomi (hoping God wouldn't punish her for saying it),

"I hate the silly little creep. You don't know how lucky you are not having a brother."

Jack crept across the landing to get a towel to dry his hair and other bits of him that were still damp. He was furious. He had never been angry with Chloe before; hurt by her, irritated by her, disappointed in her yes, but not angry. However she had never behaved like this before. She had sometimes been a bit bossy in the past, but not usually in an unkind way and he hadn't minded, had liked it even, because out of the two of them she had always been the leader and Jack, being the less inventive, had liked being led. But this was different. This was Hitler in knickers. She was being arrogant and unkind. Certainly Susan had been out of order by showing him her chest, but he didn't think that Chloe knew about that. Chloe's view of Susan as a tart was to do with the fact that her mother was single, poor and uneducated and the fact that both she and Susan dressed in a certain way. Chloe's position as a Child with Talent (she was also academically good) was going to her head. Suddenly Jack felt a surge of compassion for Susan. Back in his room again he carefully picked out some clothes – a Nike sweatshirt and some cargo pants (both bought for him by Quentin – neither Kate nor David approved of designer labels or fashion for kids) and put them on. None of his shoes which were dry were acceptable so he didn't put any on, deciding to remain barefoot. Back in the bathroom he slicked his hair with a comb then ruffled it with his hand until he got the effect he wanted. Good enough, he thought, and went downstairs.

He didn't dare go straight to the kitchen – Chloe would get him back one way or another if he made it too obviously clear that he was doing the exact opposite of what she and Naomi had told him to do. Instead he went into the lounge and switched on the telly, turning it up loud so that everyone in the house knew that he was watching it.

"Turn that DOWN!"

He turned it down and wondered how long he should wait before going into the kitchen. His fear of Susan had vanished. He couldn't possibly be afraid of someone Chloe was hunting down. With the disappearance of his fear he was able to see Susan in a neutral light now that he realised that he felt sorry for her. He hadn't forgotten what had happened between the two of them a week or two back, but it no longer particularly alarmed him. Kids their age and a bit above did that stuff all the time, it was normal. It probably just meant that she liked him, and Jack like the idea of her liking him. Maybe he would ask Sid about it. Jack was a kind boy and he began to guess at Susan's loneliness.

Jack stayed where he was for ten minutes of so while Chloe and Naomi stayed upstairs with their music playing. Then he went into the kitchen, his heart thumping a little, but determined to be bold. All of a sudden he wanted to assert himself, do what he chose without consulting or trying to please anyone else.

"Hello Susan, hello Imogen," he said as casually as he was able, although he felt really nervous. He smiled at them briefly before walking across the kitchen to get himself a drink from the fridge, then feeling that he had been quite assertive enough for one day and having made a point, he decided to go back to the television with his drink.

"Will they finished the match later?" asked Kate as he left the kitchen.

Susan kept her head down and her hands busy. She was concentrating hard on seeming unruffled.

"I don't know, I don't think so, unless they finish it tomorrow, you'll have to ask Dad."

"Do you like cricket?"

"Yes, it's great."

"Why don't you sign up for coaching if you really like it? You do need an out of school activity that you really enjoy. Has Dad suggested that?"

"No, but it's a great idea. I'll ask him about it."

That would be awesome, thought Jack. He felt so excited that he forgot himself and said,

"See you later, Susan."

Chapter 27

"This is just between the two of us. I don't want to start off an episode of Chinese Whispers."

"No problem," said Tulip. "You can rely on my discretion."

"I know," said David. "The thing is, I've almost definitely decided to give up my job, but I need another week or two to think it through."

"Give it up? Do you mean change your job for promotion or more money or something?"

"No. I really mean quite literally give it up."

Tulip sat and looked at him, uncomprehending. "You mean not work for social services anymore?"

"Yes."

"Not be a social worker anymore?"

"Yes. That's what I mean."

"Goodness. What are you going to do instead?"

"Two things. First, take in lodgers and second, help Kate start a business."

Tulip stared. "That's different. What kind of business?"

"Interior design."

For a couple of moments neither of them spoke. Then David said,

"Kate's wanted to do interior design for ages. I'm going to suggest to her that she go on a course so that she can learn how to do it properly, although at this stage I don't know if it needs to be a degree course or what. I can take a crash course in business management and accounting in the evenings and deal with that side of things. I can see now that she's just not cut out for social work. She's been trying to explain that for ages, but I wouldn't listen. I thought she was being self-indulgent but she wasn't, she was being honest and realistic. I used to think it important that we did something 'useful' in an obvious kind of way, you know, serve the community to justify our existence, make the world a better place. But now I realise it is not only the poor who are always with us, as someone once said."

"Jesus."

"What?"

"It was Jesus who said the poor will always be with us."

"Oh. Well there you are then. But now I've realised that the same is true of the emotionally damaged, the dysfunctional and the general social misfits, and I've begun to believe that all the social work in the world isn't going to change it. And I'm fed up with being ineffective, because that's how I feel at the moment."

Tulip laughed. "You're a megalomaniac, David. You're trying to be Superman and put the world to rights single-handed."

"Nonsense."

"Yes, sorry, it is nonsense. It's perfectly normal to want a sense of purpose and feel that you're achieving something worthwhile, but you have been. Look how things turned out for the Sampson family, to mention just one. If that wasn't a good result I'd like to know what was."

"True. But I've come to realise that whatever a person offers is of value, it doesn't have to be something useful in a purely concrete or utilitarian way. As someone else said, man does not live by bread alone."

"Not someone else. Same Person."

"Really? Interesting fellow."

"Quite so."

"Well, anyhow, I'm sure you've heard me say before that I think the average person should only do social work for half a lifetime. Well, that includes me. I'm an average person, not Superman at all, you see. It's different for those one or two people who are the real thing, round pegs in round holes, Polly Malone for example, she'll have been doing it for thirty-nine years when she retires next month. She was born to do it, and what results she has achieved. But the rest of us burn out sooner or later and maybe end up doing more harm than good." Polly was their director.

"Interior design is genuinely useful, for heaven's sake," said Tulip, "and not just aesthetically. Of course it's lovely to live in a visually pleasing environment, soothing to the spirit you might say, but living with badly designed things is a dreadful waste of time and money, which is to be avoided at all costs. Bad design can cause stress, accidents in the home, inefficiency and heaven knows what else."

"Agreed. But what I've recently come to realise is that even if that weren't the case, even if it were just a case of the pleasantness of living with good design, even if it wasn't also useful in a practical way, it would be enough. It took our flamboyant lodger to make me see that."

"Quentin?"

"Yes, Quentin. Until now I always saw him as an affected, stuck-up know-all, but sometimes he talks quite a lot of sense, more than I used to realise. I'm the one who's been stuck-up and arrogant and thinking I knew it all, just as much as him."

"How will you live until you get the business going?"

"Stay working for a bit. We can possibly re-mortgage later, and for that I may need to stay working here full-time for perhaps three years by which time I will be forty, and if I help Kate finish the decorating we could take up to three lodgers because we've got six bedrooms and we only need three."

"Four, with Quentin."

"Correct. But he's an awful lot better now and I think his Oxfordshire house is coming along well, it should be finished quite soon, so I should think he will want to move into it in the next few months."

David, of course, still had no idea of the real purpose behind the Oxfordshire house, or that even now Quentin had no plans to move into it yet at all. Quentin was still hedging his bets. Yes, he really felt that he was over Simon, but he was still attracted to the original plan, which had now been modified. Recently he had realised something that he had avoided facing up to before – that he might be lonely without Simon. Never mind love, never mind romance, he had never articulated to himself the bottom line of the original plan, had only just become aware of it, namely that when he was ready to move into The Studio he was hoping that Simon would stay there with him even if they were not an item, albeit as a separate entity, as just a friend.

"There are other little money-saving things" said David. "Vegetables, for example, we use loads, we're semi-vegetarian, and I already grow most of those, and what with the fruit trees and soft fruit we're well on the way to becoming self-sufficient for food. I'm thinking of taking it further by keeping chickens and maybe bees, which both give the possibility of selling the surplus. And Kate already has a bit of free-lance work design-wise – she's been so interested in it for so long that there are a few local people who pay for her advice and ideas."

"I'm speechless, David, I had no idea that all this was going on in your head."

"Well, it hasn't been for all that long, and the only reason I'm telling you about it is that when the time comes I think you ought to apply for my job."

"You're joking. What about the others – Cliff for example – surely he's miles ahead of me in the seniority stakes?"

"Well, he's certainly been in our department for longer than anyone else, but that doesn't give him seniority as such over the rest of you. If anything it's the opposite of a recommendation, because by now he ought to have risen higher through the ranks than he actually has. The fact that he hasn't says a lot about him, and even if you are not appointed it certainly won't be him. Anyhow, think about what I've said, and if you'd like to go for it let me know. I'll give you whatever help I can."

David looked at his watch. "I've got to shoot off now, I've got an appointment."

"How long have I got to think about this?"

"As long as you like within reason. As I've just said, I may make up my own mind very soon, but I'll actually be around for at least a couple of years. This is about looking ahead. I'm pretty tied up at the moment but we might get a chance to have a little chat at the street party, it's only a couple of weeks away. You are coming, aren't you?"

"Sure, wouldn't miss it for anything."

"OK, see you then if not before."

Chapter 28

"Can I help?" asked Mo, after he had watched Kate go round the DVD section of his general store for the fourth time.

"Um..." Kate felt herself blushing. She was, on the advice of both Dainty, who of late had become her confidante, and Quentin, whose opinion was usually worth having, looking for something romantic but didn't want to say so. Although Kate rarely shopped there for food or other domestic items she came in from time to time to get a DVD, usually something for the twins.

"For the kids, is it?"

"No." Mind your own business, can't you, she thought. She didn't want all the neighbours knowing what she was up to, she'd never live it down. Not that she need have worried, firstly because Mo mixed mostly only with the rest of the Indian community, and outside of his role as shopkeeper had no particular contact with those of other ethnic origins who formed most of Kate's contacts in the neighbourhood. Secondly, discretion was a quality Mo shared with Sid and Mikey, and he would no more have revealed a person's shopping habits or choice of entertainment to another customer than Sid would have said whom he saw talking to whom at three o'clock in the morning.

Kate continued to browse as Mo talked intermittently to his wife Myra – not her real name, which no one seemed to know. Myra often sat silently in the shop to one side of the counter, wrapped in a lightly woven woollen shawl, while Mo did his work. He usually spoke to her in their own language, for she knew little English. She only spoke when spoken to, and looked old enough to be Mo's mother, though she was only forty to his twenty-eight. Both families thought it a good match, his being too poor to set him up in a business at all, either in England or anywhere else, hers only able to accumulate a modest dowry, and shrewd enough to discern Mo's natural ability in matters of commerce, and his industriousness. They were not disappointed. Such marriages were not unusual where Mo and Myra came from, and she had even supplied him with two children. Cousins helped with the care of these as well as with many of the domestic arrangements. Myra, for all her silence, played the matriarch and laid down all the rules. They were a happy family.

Finally Kate thought she had found what she was looking for. It was a film called On Golden Pond starring Katherine Hepburn and Henry Fonda. The résumé on the cover suggested that it was about the healing of a relationship, that it involved emotions but wasn't too sentimental. It looked as if it could serve her purpose.

Her purpose was to encourage David. For a while it had seemed to her that because David had been so much nicer recently he wanted to revive their relationship, but now she was beginning to think that maybe he was being nicer simply because he was happier for whatever reason, and that their relationship didn't come into it. If this was the case it would be a great disappointment to Kate as, particularly after the stern talk Dainty had had with her, she had begun to feel not only relieved that the tension between herself and David was disappearing, but also increasingly excited at the possibility of being romantic again. This had all the attraction of an extramarital affair with none of the risk. Mere harmony was unsatisfactory if it wasn't going to proceed to anything more. Kate recognised the possibility that David was perhaps planning to be romantic again, but so far hadn't got round to it, and Dainty had warned, darkly, that left to their own devices men would put in the least work possible in such situations, just enough, for example, to make home a pleasanter place to be, but not enough to make their wives feel like a million dollars. She had discussed all of this at length with Dainty and more briefly with Quentin. Dainty was better than Quentin at seeing all the different angles of the situation, and loved discussing these things. With her it was an art form. It did not concern her that it was not her life, her relationship at the centre of the conversation, indeed she preferred that it were not. She was proud of her insights, and in particular her understanding of the goings-on between men and women, and she loved to help. On the other hand Quentin, historically, was definitely not someone who loved to help, even when the person to be helped was his beloved friend Kate. But he always liked to know what was going on and also to give his opinion. He did not give Kate the satisfaction of letting her go endlessly over the same ground (even though both she and Ursula had done it for him) but his pragmatic approach gave her a clarity which Dainty's complicated expositions sometimes failed to do. In any case he had mixed feelings about helping Kate to improve her marriage, as he couldn't decide whether this would be to his own advantage or not.

When David got home that evening he was clutching an expensive bunch of flowers. His chat with Tulip a couple of hours before had made him feel so much better, so much more positive and more in control of things. He felt a confidence in himself that had been absent for some considerable time. It was unburdening himself that had turned the tide. Now, if he looked back, he could see the need to do this had been building up for ages – goodness, only a few days ago he had started blurting out questions, revealing some of his innermost thoughts, to Quentin of all people. Having now done it with somebody with whom he could identify more closely than he could with Quentin, somebody he really liked and trusted, he was reaping the benefit. He could see light at the end of the tunnel and was beginning to hope for a rosy future for himself and Kate.

The house appeared to be deserted. As it happened the twins were upstairs doing their homework, as they had finally been persuaded that it was better to do it on Friday evening rather than Sunday evening, although at their age they didn't get all that much. David wandered across the hall to the kitchen, and was startled to see a stranger chopping onions on the worktop. Instead of Kate in her habitual jeans and T-shirt there stood a woman with her hair piled on top of her head wearing a white cotton blouse with a scooped-out neckline and a brightly coloured gypsy skirt, shiny tights and gold shoes of the type that Chloe wore for dancing. She turned at the sound of David's step and, almost simultaneously but not quite, David thought he recognised the woman then registered that it was in fact Kate. He wondered if she had her hair up because she had been watching that programme called Hygiene in the Kitchen that some of the women at work had been talking about, but that didn't explain what she was wearing.

"Hi, darling." He went across and kissed her on the cheek. "Been out, have you?"

"No. Oh, darling, are those for me?"

"Of course. Are you going out then?"

"No." Damn, thought Kate. I've overdone it. It's too obvious. She opened a cupboard and lifted down a vase.

Strange, thought David. She looks as though she's going out but she isn't. Never mind, better not ask any more questions. Perhaps it's the weather. It certainly is getting much warmer.

As casually as she could Kate said, "Have you got much planned for this evening?"

It was only recently that David had begun to come home relatively early on a Friday after work, so he hadn't had time to develop any particular routine.

"Not really, although I thought we might go out to dinner. Particularly as you're looking so gorgeous," he added, grabbing the opportunity to pay her a compliment.

"We can't. Dinner's nearly ready. I need warning of spontaneous events these days. I got a DVD out today though. I suddenly fancied watching one with a glass or two of wine. Will that do instead?"

"Sounds great. It's just that I want to have a little chat with you – just you and me. But a DVD's fine. Are the twins going to watch it?"

"I don't know, it's up to them, I think they might. What did you want to have a little chat about?"

"About you going to college to study interior design."

She stared at him. "But you don't approve of interior design."

"That was before. I'm a changed man. I want you to be happy. I've been stupid."

"I'd love to. I'd really love to."

"That's settled then. We'll go out to dinner tomorrow and talk about it. I'll book a table and the other members of the household can make their own eating arrangements. It'll do them the world of good. Shall I go and get the wine for this evening now?"

"It's OK. I've got it already. The usual. I got two bottles actually in case Quentin wants some, although he probably won't want to watch the movie. I know how much you two can get through once you get started."

"Oh. Well, what with Quentin maybe and the twins it doesn't look as though it's going to be a cosy little twosome then, does it?"

However David said this without any sign of rancour. There had been a time when the idea of Quentin joining them would have really irritated him, but he was feeling so good and everything was unfolding so nicely that he really didn't mind at all. In fact it would give him a chance to show how pleasant he could be, including with Quentin.

In the event Quentin and the twins did watch the movie with them. Kate drank more than she normally would, and David and Quentin for some reason considerably less. As a result the diaphanous new nightdress that Kate had left lying on the bed triggered the result that she had been hoping for.

Chapter 29

"What happened to good old Lyons Corner House," moaned Quentin. He didn't like Starbucks.

All the same they had managed to find a table, something which became increasingly difficult in London as the year wore on. As the height of summer approached the volume of visitors in the capital increased daily, and Quentin refused to have coffee at all if he would have to sit on a bar stool to drink it. In the absence of Lyons he preferred to have his morning coffee and afternoon tea at Fortnum and Mason or the National Gallery, although Ursula wasn't so fussy.

"You're such a miserable old reactionary," she said, "Starbuck's coffee is loads better than the rubbish you used to get at Lyons."

"I didn't know you were old enough to remember," said Quentin. "I was only about fourteen myself when they finally closed, but it was about the ambience more than the coffee."

"That was because your immaturity was seduced by the false glamour of the place."

They were both exceptionally cheerful. There was an expectancy and muted excitement in the air that was always part of being in London at this time of year, particularly during such glorious weather, what with the increase in the influx of tourists and folk in general seeming in holiday mood. There were, however, other reasons. The editing of Quentin's paper was all but finished. This was a source of relief and satisfaction to both of them. Ursula, pleased with the paper both for its own sake but also for Quentin's, was cautiously hopeful that Quentin really was cured, though the thought that Simon would be at the street party was still causing her anxiety. She was still annoyed with Kate, who seemed oblivious even now of the possible dangers. Ursula knew nothing of the personal angst Kate had been experiencing until recently. However Quentin's obvious fascination with Natasha showed Ursula that there was a new idea in Quentin competing with the idea of Simon, something that could command his attention and satisfy his need for affirmation, although she was hoping that the original obsession wasn't going to be replaced by a different one. It meant with any luck that if Quentin's feeling ran too high in connection with Simon at the street party then Natasha could be used as a distraction.

Natasha's arrival on the scene was causing Ursula occasional pangs of jealousy but the reasonable part of her mind, which was most of it, reassured her that it was no more logical to be jealous of Natasha than of Simon – common sense showed that they were both equally unobtainable from Quentin's point of view. Ursula could hardly imagine Natasha, the way she had been described, wanting Quentin for herself.

"We had a letter from Natasha yesterday," Quentin offered brightly.

"We?"

"Yes, well the envelope was addressed to Kate but inside it there was a little piece written to each of us, even the twins!"

"How cute. What did your bit say?"

"I can't remember the exact words but it was something along the lines of how nice it had been to meet me and that she was looking forward to seeing me again at the street party, and that maybe we could spend some time together once she begins her studies at Bristol University, because although she's doing media studies herself she thinks archaeology must be very interesting."

Ursula didn't like the sound of this too much.

"How touching. But fancy someone choosing to go to Bristol when they could have gone to Oxford."

"She *is* quite eccentric, but she's an absolute delight."

"Maybe it takes one to appreciate one."

"One what?"

"Eccentric. Will she be going into hall?"

"I'm not sure. There's been a kind of background talk at The Grange about Natasha renting a room there. I must say it bothers me slightly. A change in the status quo that one hasn't chosen oneself is always a bit alarming."

It sounded a bit alarming to Ursula too, but she said, "Only to you, my darling Quentin. You're so paranoid." It gave her a delicious secret thrill to say 'my darling Quentin' in this disguised way, offering it as a style of speaking whilst satisfying her desire to say these precise words to him.

"Yes, but if she does come to stay, it could mean that they won't want me there any more. They have got six bedrooms though, so maybe I *am* being paranoid."

Ursula was thinking. On one hand, if Quentin was still vulnerable on the Simon front she had, till now, thought he would be better staying on a bit longer at the Dawsons. But did that still hold good if Natasha was living at The Grange?

"What about the Oxfordshire house? Won't you be moving in there in the not so distant future? Surely it's almost finished now. What else is there still left to do?"

"Not a lot, certainly. It's mostly just decoration waiting to be done now. There are a few other bits and pieces to do – the mouldings on the kitchen units need a bit of fiddling with, for example, and the odd bit of architrave and skirting board hasn't been done, and I'm still waiting, for the ceiling roses for the bedrooms – they've been on order for ages. It could actually be another six months before the house is actually ready to move into."

"Rubbish. All of those things could be done after you move in."

"I want it completely finished before I move in," said Quentin obstinately. "If small details are left until afterwards there's a good chance they'll never get done at all."

He was beginning to feel rather tense. They were getting onto dangerous ground here. Ursula, of course, had absolutely no idea that he was still planning for Simon to go and live in the house any more than anyone else did, for in spite of the considerable improvement in Quentin's spirits these days this was still the plan – unless the street party proved to Quentin in his own mind that he no longer wanted to be around Simon at all, or that Simon was equally keen to stay away from him. He feared that deprived of a relationship of some kind with the safety net that was Natasha, although he wasn't expecting this, his emotions would very likely swing back to Simon.

"Necessity is the mother of a lot of things," said Ursula. "If you were forced to move out of The Grange you could move into the Oxfordshire house tomorrow if you had to, couldn't you? I mean are all the services, you know, the drains and electricity and such, all in place and working?"

"I think so," said Quentin. His stomach was knotting up and he was beginning to panic. He had not foreseen anything like this – namely, Ursula, Kate or David putting him on the spot, asking for details of his move from The Grange to the renovated house in terms of the how and when. His innate craftiness came to his aid.

"The services may all be in place but of course it's still only May so the winter's not far behind us, and as The Studio, as a house, hasn't been lived in as such for something like eight or ten years it will obviously need a great deal of airing out, you know, with open windows and doors when it's warm and sunny or the central heating on if we have any cold, wet days in the summer. Otherwise it could have a detrimental effect on my health."

"Did I hear you say 'The Studio'?"

"Yes. That's going to be the name of the house. What do you think of it?"

"I don't know. It seems a bit odd for a rambling stone country house."

"That's half the point. Heaven forbid that I should be found guilty of mundanity."

He forbore to inform her that the other half of the point was that in fact it was going to be a studio – Simon's. "Of course I'll have to inform the Post Office that I've changed the name but I don't foresee any problems on that count."

"What was it called before?"

"Chez Nous."

"Oh."

There was not a lot more that Ursula could say, to Quentin's relief, because he had suddenly become afraid that she would guess what his plans were. Nevertheless he was feeling a lot more subdued than he had half an hour or so earlier. He was very fond of Ursula, and if it wasn't for her there was no knowing how or where he might have ended up, but now he felt that she was interfering too much in his life. Her wishes in connection with the details of his immediate future seemed set on a collision course with his own.

"Are you all right, Quentin? You're looking a bit odd."

"Of course, I'm fine," he said hastily.

Ursula decided to backpedal a bit. On the face of it, a few moments ago she had thought that she would rather that Quentin moved out of The Grange if Natasha was going to be moving in, just to be on the safe side. She now thought that maybe, from the point of view of the unknown effect that meeting Simon again after all this time might have on him he would be safer at The Grange till the street party was over, and Natasha's presence would increase the safety factor.

Additionally, at The Grange anything that occurred between Quentin and Natasha would be chaperoned by the Dawsons. This could not be the case once he had moved into The Studio where, since the pair of them obviously intended to be friends, Natasha was very likely to find herself overnighting after various evening functions that they might well attend together. Ursula was decidedly uncomfortable with that idea. The first time it might just be for convenience, but who knows what it could lead to?

"On second thoughts I think it would be best if you stayed a bit longer at the Dawsons if it's all right with them, say till New Year. It's already the end of May and let's face it, they have got the space. You're right about the details of houses never getting finished if you don't do them at the time. It often happens. And although you may not like me mentioning it or agree with me, I think you'd certainly best stay there until after the street party. I'm still not sure how you're going to react at seeing Simon again and let's face it, neither are you. Best to play it safe."

"Just what I think myself," said Quentin.

Chapter 30

There were eleven days left until the Big Day.

I think I can get just one more on that corner, thought Kate. She squeezed the icing bag again and out came the final pink rose onto the corner of the sheet of greaseproof paper. She looked at the clock. It was half past eleven, and David had already gone to bed. She wondered whether he was still reading or if he had gone to sleep. There were now as many red and pink roses as she would need and she toyed with the idea of doing the yellow ones as well so as to get the job finished, but decided against it.

Just as she was putting her piping equipment into the sink there was a sudden violent banging at the front door and the bell was rung several times in quick succession. Kate froze in shock. What was it? An emergency? A few seconds passed, then pulling herself together she was just about to go and see if she could discover who it was without opening the door when it came again. In panic Kate rushed out of the kitchen and began running upstairs to get David only to meet him on his way down, two steps at a time.

He pushed her aside and went to the door.

"Who the hell is it?" he yelled, without opening it.

Kate heard a woman's voice but couldn't distinguish the words she said. She thought she sounded drunk. David looked shocked. Then he said,

"What the hell do you want at this time of night?"

The banging and ringing started again.

"Open the door, for heaven's sake," said Kate, "she'll wake the whole house."

"She already has," said Quentin, who had arrived at the top of the stairs, followed by the twins. David opened the door and in fell Tracy. Her hair was tousled, her make-up smudged and she could hardly stand. She groped for the wall and propped herself against it.

"You're drunk," said David, stating the obvious. "How did you get here?"

"Tom dropped me off." Her speech was almost incomprehensible.

"What for?"

"I asked him to. I wanted to see you."

At this point Tracy slid down the wall against which she was leaning and ended up sitting on the floor. David was horrified. This could have irreparable repercussions if he failed to bluff it out.

"You're very drunk and I'm going to take you home. We'll talk about this in my office on Monday morning."

"No you're not," said Kate, "I mean you're not going to take her home. I'd like to know what's going on. She can get a taxi. Quentin, be a dear and take the twins into the kitchen and make them a hot drink."

Thankfully Tracy had fallen asleep.

"We can't put her in a taxi, she's far too drunk. I'll have to take her myself."

"In that case I'm coming with you. You'll need help anyway. She'll be a dead weight if she doesn't come round. You'll never manage on your own."

"That's true. But it would be better if I took Quentin. He's a man." David was close to panic, and if Tracy had anything else to say he didn't want Kate to hear it.

"No. He's fine looking after the twins. I'll come myself."

Kate went into the kitchen to speak to Quentin, then she and David manhandled the semi-conscious Tracy into the car.

The short journey was uneventful.

"I didn't know you had any of your staff living this close to us," said Kate icily as they pulled up outside Tracy's flat in Balmoral Road.

"I had no reason to mention it," sighed David. "It's hardly of major interest."

"Funny how you didn't need to ask her the address."

"Just as well in the circumstances, don't you think? I know the addresses of all my staff and have given lifts home to several at one time or another."

Kate was suddenly smitten with intense fatigue and chose not to invite him to elaborate. After years of feeling alienated from Kate David had developed rapid reflexes and also low cunning – he was now covered for the unlikely eventuality of either Sid or Mikey making any kind of tactless observation.

David pulled up outside Tracy's ground floor flat and Kate located her key. They bundled her out of the car and through the door into the house. The idea of helping her to bed had occurred to and been rejected by each of them separately without being verbalised, so they left her in a heap on the hall floor, put the key in her bag, slammed the door behind them and departed.

When they got home the lights were all blazing but the house was in silence. Quentin and the twins had gone back to bed.

"I'll sleep in the guest room," said Kate evenly. She was so fed up with the whole thing that she couldn't even be bothered to make a fuss any more, though she intended to put David through it later. "I've got a cracking headache and if I'm tossing and turning it'll only keep you awake."

"Okay," said David. It suited him fine. He too preferred to spend the night alone to have the chance of thinking through whatever strategy might be required.

Chapter 31

"Have another, old chap," said Quentin, "it'll do you good."

"Thanks. Could you make it a double?"

David and Quentin didn't normally drink together in the Sceptre even though it was their local, in fact they had rarely drunk together at all. However desperate times produce all kinds of unexpected turns, and Quentin was frantic. For three days now he had watched his dear friend Kate moping around the house, pale and withdrawn. She was unhappier than he had ever seen her and it was distressing him terribly. What made it worse was that she refused to talk to him. He knew of course that this was simply because she was so unhappy and not because he had upset her himself, but Kate closed down completely when she was feeling bad, and for once in his life Quentin felt so miserable about it all that he had a need to do something. She wouldn't come out with him for a drink, so he had invited David out for one instead. Quentin hoped Kate wouldn't see this as disloyalty, but at least he might get a handle on the whole thing if he discovered what David's story was.

It was only now that Quentin had come to realise just how bad David himself, who had clearly been out of sorts to some degree for the same length of time as Kate, was feeling. Quentin had been vaguely aware that David had not been at home much over the past few days, and when he had he had been quiet and morose. He was also aware that some undefined relationship between David and Tracy was the issue at stake, and Quentin himself had no real idea as to whether it was about the kind of trivial flirtation that routinely occurs in office situations or something more substantial.

After only half an hour in the pub they had already had two, and now Quentin was going up to get the third. Whatever it takes, he thought, and after all if this was his own chosen method of dealing with severe pain, why shouldn't it be David's? Quentin's reaction to the situation was not entirely an altruistic response to Kate's suffering but was also due to his determination that nothing, but nothing was going to prevent the street party from taking place if there was anything he could do about it. No street party equalled no Natasha, at least not for a while, and worse still, no Simon. Natasha would reappear at some point anyway, but the street party was possibly his last chance of dignified closure with Simon romantically as well as the only opportunity of securing him as a long term but platonic companion. So although it was probably true that Quentin's main concern was in fact for himself, this helped him considerably in giving the traumatised David his full attention.

"Look, old chap, the situation's not irretrievable. You've just got to give it time. She'll come round."

"I don't know. She might or she might not. I really don't know. I can't bear it." David began to cry.

Shyly, Quentin put his arm round David's shoulders and patted him gently.

"I know what you're going through," he said with genuine feeling. "However, as a matter of interest, was there actually anything going on between you and this Tracy?"

"Not a lot. I started giving her a lift home after the Friday night meetings simply because she lives just round the corner. Then I began to realise that she found me attractive and I suppose I was flattered. Then it kind of, well, you know, went on from there. Not much happened really, just a bit of groping and suchlike, but it certainly would have gone further if I hadn't suddenly come to my senses. The silly thing is, I can see now that I don't much like her, let alone fancy her. Kate and I haven't been getting on for a long time. We just seem to have drifted apart. I didn't feel I was important to her anymore. Then another female starts making me think that she thinks I'm the bee's knees and for a while I enjoyed that until I realised what the implications were and what the outcome could be. That's when I realised that it was up to me to put more into my marriage. It was working until Tracy turned up the other night."

Quentin was beginning to enjoy himself. David had stopped crying after a few minutes and was becoming quite mellow as the alcohol increasingly took hold. Quentin was finding that to be the counsellor rather than the counselled was quite appealing. It certainly felt more dignified. The resulting sense of slight superiority disposed him to be kind to David, in fact it was changing his attitude to David quite dramatically. He had always seen David as being quite without any kind of vulnerability, devoid of any emotion, and cold, dull and selfish. But as the alcohol flowed and David became increasingly chatty a quite different person was emerging. Quentin heard about the little boy who had grown up on a large council estate and whose father was permanently enraged at the injustice in the world. Not, as you might suppose from the depths of his fury, at the unforgivable injustice which allows babies to die of hunger and disease, but the injustice which allowed some men to have large private houses while others lived in dreary council accommodation, which allowed some men to have shiny new cars and well-dressed wives whilst others with rather dowdier wives were obliged to take the bus, which allowed David's father's brother, who had always been the favourite with David's grandparents, to have his own thriving and highly profitable building firm, whilst David's father himself, more often than not, was unemployed.

"What did he used to do all day?" asked Quentin.

"I'm not absolutely sure, but when he wasn't in the pub shooting his mouth off he was often out buying and selling things. He had ideas about getting into the antique dealing business. And I can remember various attempts at breeding. Once it was budgerigars, another time it was Persian cats. At the time I really believed that he had been unlucky and badly treated, and that it was my job to put things right by changing the world, but I don't believe either of those things now, although I still believed the second until quite recently. When he died five years ago I didn't feel any grief at all. I was just relieved that my mother would perhaps finally be able to get a bit of peace and happiness for a few years. Actually I think she is. She's got a granny annexe now in my uncle's enormous house. They all seem to get on well together."

They sat in silence for a while, each of them lost in his own thoughts. Each was surprise to find that, after all, the other seemed to be quite a decent chap. Eventually David said,

"It was good of you to ask me out, Quentin, it really was. I hadn't realised how much I needed someone to talk to. I haven't really got anyone else, except for Tulip."

"Don't mention it, old boy." Quentin felt like hugging David, but thought better of it. Another time perhaps, he thought. Rome wasn't built in a day.

Chapter 32

Mikey didn't work on Sundays. Most Sunday mornings he went to the Methodist Church along with the more traditional of the Cannon Street believers, and then to the rather more rousing Pentecostal Church, where the music was more his kind of thing, on Sunday evening. Sometimes he did it the other way round. He could always be sure of seeing Sid at the first, with or without Wendy, and Amos at the second, always with Dainty but never with Piety. In about an hour's time Mikey and Joe would be making their way towards the Pentecostal Church for the evening service.

Right now, however, they were scampering across the landing every two or three minutes or so, clad only in boxer shorts, first into Joe's room, then out again and into Mikey's, then back again into Joe's. Both their beds were piled high with clothing.

Joe put on a pair of green and black skin-tight striped trousers together with a red shirt, gold waistcoat and blue bow tie.

"What d' you think?"

"Not bad. What d' you think of this?" Mikey had put on black leather trousers, a white T-shirt and a black tail coat.

"Cool. But better for an evening do than daytime. It might be okay though if it's not too warm."

They were deciding what to wear for the street party in two days' time. Up and down the length of Cannon Street others were doing exactly the same thing.

"Is you girlfriend coming, may I make so bold as to ask?"

"What girlfriend? I haven't got a girlfriend."

Mikey stared at him. He had seen Joe and Ellen and Alan and Becky at the Dugout for five weekends in a row now, and also knew that they regularly played snooker at Blues in a foursome.

"I mean Ellen. Heavens, man, ain't you scored yet?" ' Scored', with Mikey, had a relatively innocuous meaning.

"I haven't been trying to."

"You're kidding. I've seen you together every week."

"Alan's the one who's after her, not me."

"Don't tell me that, man. She's gorgeous, can't you see that?"

"Well, yes, I can see that, but I can't nick me mate's bird. Although he hasn't scored yet either, come to think of it. He's really shy, and I'm not sure she wants a relationship now anyway. I don't either, come to that."

"Oh, man." Mikey was really disappointed, but he didn't want to let Joe know how much.

"I'll have a girlfriend eventually, I just can't do it like my friends, a different girl every couple of weeks, it looks exhausting. I want a soul mate. Nothing else will do. Anyway, what's the rush? You aiming to be a grandpa soon or what?"

"That would be awesome."

Joe laughed. "Bide your time, then, like for ten or fifteen years, and you might get lucky. Once I'm off to uni, though, you could marry Topaz. She must be sick of waiting for me to get out of the way."

"Topaz isn't the one. We're just good friends."

Joe gave him an old fashioned look. "You could've fooled me."

Mikey laughed. "Us older folk are much more restrained in our relationships than you youngsters. Believe half of what you see and nothing of what you hear."

"Sure. Come on, let's get dressed or we'll be late."

Chapter 33

To some the street party was just another local opportunity to eat, drink and be merry, if not to get downright plastered with an official excuse. For others it was an historic occasion worthy of extravagant but dignified celebration, and in the forefront of these was Kate and her band of helpers. For yet others it was an opportunity to take centre stage, whether as a visual exhibit with the most stylish appearance, like Imogen, or from a racy or controversially high profile, like Piety. Again, there were those, like Kathleen and Mikey, who were simply looking forward to intermingling and enjoying the company of friends and neighbours.

The day before the party Imogen and Piety found themselves sitting next to each other in Mikey's Unisex Hair Salon, and Mikey had a dilemma. He had booked in too many people, more through his wish to avoid disappointing anybody than with an eye to profit. He knew of course that Piety was pregnant, and he had recently heard that Imogen was too. He knew that Wendy wanted to be and wasn't, and fearing an emotional scene on such a busy day he was reluctant to ask her to work on either of these two clients, and was wondering if he himself could do both women at the same time. He had his two part-timers in for the whole day, because although many of the revellers-to-be had been done on Saturday and, for once, yesterday, Sunday, the Monday appointment page was still choc-a bloc. The part-timers were working flat out. Three ladies were reading magazines in the waiting area. One of them had been there for over half an hour, and Piecrust, the school caretaker, would be in in a minute and wouldn't let anyone but Mikey do the tracery through his hair. Mikey sighed and went over to Wendy, who was just taking old Mrs Roderick's rollers out.

"Sorry, love, I know neither of them is booked in with you, but when you've finished Mrs Roderick could you go and start either Imogen or Piety? We're beginning to run late, and if we're not careful we'll never get out of here before bedtime."

Mikey was apprehensive. He had hardly spoken to Wendy today, there simply hadn't been time, and what with her feeling so broody he had absolutely no idea what mood she was in.

He was quite startled when she turned towards him a countenance of utter radiance and smiled.

"No problem," she said. "I've got a slight lull, so I can start them both if you like."

"Fantastic. I can do one of them, Piety probably, if you can just get them both shampooed."

Wendy smiled again. "Consider it done."

Imogen and Piety meanwhile were sitting in silence in their adjacent chairs with capes round their shoulders and scrutinising themselves in the mirrors. Piety liked what she saw – the whole face so much slimmer than her sister's, its large, wide-spaced eyes, the full, inviting mouth and the straight nose inherited from a distant ancestor of East Indian origin. The hair, certainly, looked a bit like a bird's nest, but at five and a half months her pregnancy was becoming uncomfortable and she wasn't sleeping well. Also the Sceptre had been busy lately which meant that Dainty had not been available for the six-weekly unplaiting and re-plaiting chore. However within an hour or two Piety would be ready for the big day.

Imogen was feeling anxious about her appearance. Hairdressing salons always had this effect on her. In the strategically placed mirrors in her own home she always looked good providing she had made the effort with her naturally bright complexion, regular, well-balanced features, and the fine, flyaway hair which made her reminiscent of a mythological nymph. Salon mirrors, conversely, were not strategically placed, or if they were it was not in a way likely to flatter the client. Gloomily Imogen stared at a narrow, rat-like face with deep nose to mouth lines, dull, coarse skin, lank hair and a downturned mouth. She wondered whether she should book herself in for a perm next time to give her hair a lift.

"What you gonna have done?"

Imogen turned her face toward her neighbour.

"I'm not sure. I've had it the way it is now since I was about six. I've never found anything else that works. It just seems to be that sort of hair."

"You should have it short and spiky."

"Oh, I couldn't. Shane would hate it. It wouldn't be feminine."

"Nonsense. Short hair's real sexy. Men hate long hair. It's restrictive, know what I mean? Either you are lying on it or he is lying on it."

"What are you having done?" asked Imogen, hastily changing the subject.

"Real short, with tracery. I'm too far gone to sit for six, seven hours being unplaited and re-plaited."

"Really? I thought tracery was just for boys and men."

"Well, that's probably what they think too." Piety threw back her head and laughed. "I'm real proud of my bump, but while I got no figure I want some other kind of eye-catching t'ing."

Imogen was intrigued. She was enjoying Piety. She had rarely had a female friend.

"Have you got a name for your baby?" asked Imogen.

"Peppermint if it's a girl, Pitcher if it's a boy."

Imogen wondered why Caribbean people gave their children such strange names.

"You don't know which it is, then?"

"Nope, and I don't want to. It ain't natural. A person didn't oughta know if it's a boy or a girl before it's born."

"I think that too. My names are Anthony or Gillian."

Neither of them had noticed that Wendy had come up to stand behind them.

"Good morning, ladies. I like flower names for girls, I've decided, and biblical names for boys. How can I help?"

Imogen jumped. Piety smiled.

"Are we talking babies' names or hairstyles?"

"Hairstyles."

"Is it okay to have Mikey do mine? No offence."

"None taken. I know he always does yours. But would you like me to shampoo it first? It would save time."

"Okay. Mind you use the coconut shampoo."

"Of course. How about you, Imogen?"

"I really can't decide how to have it, but I'm really fed up with the way it looks now."

"I'll bring you the book. You might find something in there that you like."

As she went to fetch the book Piety said in a stage whisper:

"She's pregnant."

Imogen was surprised.

"Really? I didn't know that."

"Most people don't. I don't know if she does herself."

"So how do you know?"

"Easy. She's got the look. It's in the voice as well. And talking 'bout babies' names."

Mikey arrived before Wendy came back.

"When's the wedding then, Piety? Time's running out if that baby's gonna be legitimate."

"Legitimate? What's with legitimate? Move on Mikey, these is modern times. Anyways, who would you have me marry?"

"How about the father of the baby? Know who it is?"

"What's it to you, man? We both know it ain't you."

Mikey laughed. "You heathen. A baby's better off with two parents, preferably married. To each other."

"Ain't too many babies with married to each other parents where I come from. Where I come from a baby might have any number of parents between one and fifteen, but two, now that's the most unusual."

Wendy returned with a jumbo bottle of coconut shampoo – they got through gallons of it at Mikey's - and a book full of styles for Imogen to look at. She flicked through the book rapidly until she came to a certain page, then put it in Imogen's lap.

"There's one you might like," she said. "That short, spiky style would look fabulous on you."

Chapter 34

The big day dawned grey but dry and everything was more or less ready. By seven in the morning David, Mikey, Shane and Amos were already hard at work getting the tables and chairs, which had been procured from various sources, out of the Dawson's garden shed and into the street. Mikey, Shane and Amos were in buoyant mood, and this helped David a lot. He felt listless and depressed but not panic-stricken, as he had a few days ago. Immediately after the Tracy episode he had feared that Kate might simply walk out, and the thought had terrified him. Now, however, ten days or so down the line, she was still here, in body if not in spirit, which suggested that she wasn't planning to leave, not for the moment at least. Maybe she had only decided to hang on for the street party, in order not to let everyone down, but David had decided not to think about that and was taking the view that as long as she was actually here he was in with a chance. The difficulty was that she wouldn't speak to him so he had had no opportunity to defend himself or explain or find out what she was thinking. She wasn't speaking to anyone else either as far as he knew. She had taken to avoiding David physically as much as she could, leaving a room the minute he entered it. If there was something she really needed to say to him, where possible she communicated it through other people. Home was calm but tense. Now, though, the camaraderie and banter were keeping him going and even began to lift his spirits a little, and it occurred to him that Kate would find it difficult to avoid him totally for the whole day and that maybe, during it, he would find a way of beginning a healing process for their relationship. The abundant availability of alcohol was a bit of a wild card which could tip the situation either way.

Kate, meanwhile, was in the kitchen. She looked awful. The huge grey bags under her eyes were testimony to the fact that she had hardly slept for over a week. Her lips were the same shade as the rest of her face, which was ashen, and her hair, which she hadn't brushed for two or three days, was by now matted rather than tousled. It was as much as she could be bothered to do to comb it through roughly with her fingers. She hadn't left the house during that time because it hadn't really been necessary. Everything except last minute perishables had been laid in for days, and she sent Quentin and the twins out to get those.

What got to her most was the feeling of having been duped. If her relationship with David had still been the same as it was a year ago this episode wouldn't have affected her nearly as much. She might not even have cared; she would probably have seen it as extra ammunition to use against him. She might even have been glad; she would have felt justified then had she decided to leave him. But now, after a month of the new David, who seemed to care about their marriage, about her and the twins, and after almost a fortnight of she herself trusting, responding in kind, it was unbearable. She thought of the new nightdresses she had bought, two of which were still in their tissue paper, and burst into tears just as Dainty walked in through the kitchen door. Dainty put her arms round Kate's shoulders.

"Come on, honey, it's all part of the package. Let's get on with the day."

"What do you mean, all part of the package?" asked Kate through a sob.

"I mean there's a reverse side to every coin. The down side of caring 'bout someone more is that you gonna be more hurt when things go wrong. When are the other food helpers arriving?"

"Ten o'clock. You're two and a half hours early."

"I know. It was deliberate. I wanted to get to you first. Why have you been refusing to see me or talk to me on the phone?"

"I've been feeling so rotten. I haven't wanted to see or talk to anybody."

"It's just that you've been feeling so angry, and because you're so enjoying your righteous indignation and wallowing in your pain that you don't want people like me coming round and talking you out of it."

Dainty had an idea of what had happened from the things Shane and Imogen, who lived opposite and had heard the commotion, had said in the pub the day after.

"That's not fair."

"But it's true. The fact that you are hurting dreadfully doesn't alter that. Let's put the kettle on and have a cup of tea. We need to straighten you out a bit before the others get here. You look awful."

It was a great relief to Kate that Dainty was taking over. Today she really didn't have the energy to keep all the balls in the air without help. She would have cancelled the party had it been possible, but in spite of the pain she had been in she could not allow herself to disappoint so many people. Dainty knew this, and thought that Kate had done well to keep going.

They had a cup of tea, then Dainty sent Kate upstairs to tidy herself up. She came down three quarters of an hour later looking almost reasonable thanks to a more liberal than usual application of make-up.

By the time Kate got back down to the kitchen Dainty had made a list of the order of play so that once the other helpers arrived they would simply have to execute the plan. She put some coffee on to brew then sat down at the kitchen table with Kate.

"Now, tell me exactly what happened."

Kate told her.

"So when you interrogated David the next morning he finally admitted that there had been a minor flirtation between them?"

"Yes."

"He said there had been no actual sex or anything remotely approaching it?"

"Yes."

"So what's the problem you're left with? What does it signify to you that your husband made a mistake and had a minor flirtation with a colleague which, if I've understood you correctly, is over?"

Kate began to get indignant. "It signifies that I and my children and, for what it's worth, Quentin were, through my husband's bad behaviour, subjected to a traumatic and humiliating experience in our own home."

"That's the result of the mistake, not the significance of it."

"Okay. It signifies that he's an arsehole."

"Fine. Are you implying that you can only stay married to someone who never ever behaves like an arsehole or makes a mistake?"

"But he let me think our relationship was improving."

"It was. It has been. He was simply caught out, as tends to happen, by the consequences of his previous behaviour. He has been completely consistent from well before the day Natasha first arrived in working at your marriage. He didn't ask Tracy to come round drunk."

Kate remained silent.

"Has David apologised?"

"Kind of. He tried two or three times."

"But you didn't accept his apology?"

"No. I told him to naff off."

"Have you given him a chance to explain?"

"No."

"Have you decided in advance that no explanation and no apology, however genuine, will be adequate?"

Kate hesitated. "Maybe."

"Why?"

"He's made a fool of me and hurt my feelings."

"So are you going to continue in a marriage where you have a permanent grudge against your husband and expect him to do the same, just because of your vanity?"

Kate hesitated, then said, "That won't work, will it?"

"No, it won't."

"What am I going to do then?"

"Let him apologise and accept his apology provided he promises never to do such a thing again, unless you are willing to let your marriage go."

"I don't feel like it right now."

"Do it anyway."

There was a long silence.

"Okay."

"Now I want you to put this out of your mind and not ruin the day for everyone else. Okay?"

"Okay."

Chapter 35

Quentin felt like a small child again. He had the feeling he had had long ago when, waking before the break of dawn he suddenly realised that today was his sixth, his seventh, his eighth birthday. He was restless with anticipation. This was the big day. He was at last going to see Simon. A little voice in his head said "Be careful!" and at first he ignored it. Today he was going to have a good time. Today he was going to prove to himself and anyone else who had noticed his dependency that he had reclaimed his own life. Today he was going to demonstrate that addiction had been conquered and his sense of himself as a sane, rational human being recovered.

He had come to see that he and Simon were not going to spend the rest of their lives together. He was now astonished at his long-term belief that they might do so. Meeting Natasha had made him see that there was an infinite number of possible relationships, some more desirable than others, some more workable than others, waiting out there in the world. He had become more aware of Simon's inability to offer him anything other than a casual friendship than of his desirability. At this moment in time he couldn't care less about this. He simply wanted to be carefree again, and had begun to think about what fun it would be to start a new relationship, even though there were no obvious candidates at the moment. This idea vanquished any feelings of disappointment that something was coming to an end, and highlighted the fact that in reality his relationship with Simon, other than as a tenuous acquaintance, had ended three years ago. Nevertheless he thought that maybe he should heed the warning inner voice that he had heard when he awoke. He remembered the other times he had though he was back in control: the telephone call of two years ago, and the more recent calls he had made to Simon's number since he had been living with the Dawsons. Maybe there was still some part of him emotionally that could be drawn back to the dangerous pre-worn path if he wasn't sufficiently vigilant.

At a quarter to five Quentin went down to the kitchen to make himself a cup of tea. It was already fairly light. The kettle was hot, as he expected. He had heard someone go downstairs a little earlier. Back in his room and propped up in bed with several cushions he sipped his tea slowly, wallowing in the anticipation of the day that was just beginning. He felt light-headed and unreal. A little later he crept back downstairs for his second cup, taking with him a pen and a pad of writing paper. He would write a poem. It would be a symbol of a break with the past and a new beginning. He thought he would try a bit of haiku. It was short, and not difficult, surely, though he could never remember all the minutely detailed rules:

The beautiful youth
Smiled kindly at his old friend,

And stroked his pale cheek

Obscure and pretentious, thought Quentin. Perfect, even if technically incorrect. Sounds of movement had begun upstairs, so he quickly closed the pad, made himself some more tea and took the steaming mug, the pen and the paper back up to his room. Then he set about rustling through his wardrobe to find some suitably striking party attire.

Chapter 36

Other guests and the organisers of the Cannon Street Queen's Golden Jubilee Street Party were preparing for the day in their different ways. Whilst the men laid out trestle tables Kate, still depressed, was drifting around the kitchen and Quentin had begun to examine the contents of his wardrobe. Susan was laying up a breakfast tray, complete with little posy, for her mother. Imogen, needless to say, was still asleep. Because of this Susan would not be able to prepare the actual food for another couple of hours at least. She was the happiest she had ever been. She had had a great time at the fair with Shane, who had been unrestrainedly indulgent with her. They had talked a lot, and Susan was beginning to see things differently. A few weeks ago she had been feeling angry with her mother, but now she really felt she wanted to give her a treat.

Sheila, too, was exceptionally happy. Things were working out so well between her and Simon, and she was really looking forward to meeting this family who actually were, as she had suspected, Natasha's relatives. As Susan was putting the bread in the toaster for her mother's breakfast Sheila and Natasha were getting on the train. Making the journey with her friend was the icing on the cake for Sheila.

Simon had a sense of good things to come. He felt a deep gratitude that his relationship with his sister had been renewed. Many times over the years he had thought that he might have lost her for ever, and that she would carry a tarnished image of him with her throughout her life. They had talked over what had happened many times, and Sheila had kept reassuring him that Denise had forgiven him, indeed that it probably didn't occur to her that there was anything to forgive. Now Simon had begun to forgive himself, and this was helping to take the tension out of the Quentin situation. He now felt able, if the opportunity cropped up, to explain everything to Quentin and ask his forgiveness too, although he could see that in some ways Quentin was the author of his own misfortune.

Breakfast time on Jubilee Party morning threw up (quite literally) some anxiety in the Farmer household. Wendy had been vomiting. Sid was concerned (even he had the day off – there had been a double drop on both Saturday and Monday) and wanted to call the emergency doctor but Wendy, who had secretly been to the doctor the previous week, refused and insisted on getting dressed up for the street party. An hour or so later she was feeling much better.

"You had me worried for a minute," said Sid, relieved. "It must have been a touch of summer tummy."

"It wasn't," she said, grinning. "I'm expecting."

Sid stared at her, his mouth open.

"Well say something then."

Silently he took her in his arms and laid his cheek against hers. They stood like that for some minutes, then he said,

"I can't believe it. I simply can't believe it," then kissed her and hugged her some more.

Tulip had been out for her customary early morning walk. Now she sat eating rye crispbread thickly spread with apricot compote and drinking herb tea. She wasn't a health freak, nevertheless thought it wise to put herself in with a chance of staying the course. People from where she came from, and their friends, really knew how to celebrate.

Tracy had a compound hangover. In recent days she had been out drinking every lunch time and every night. She was feeling belligerent. Everyone seemed to have a boyfriend except her. There was a pimply youth at her local pub who was pursuing her. He was a butcher's apprentice and still lived with his mother, and much too naff for Tracy to consider taking him on. She was hoping the street party would throw up a suitable mate for her. This may have been unrealistic, but at the moment optimism was about the only thing she had going for her, and at least there would be plenty of free booze around. Her recent excesses had made quite a hole in her pocket.

Tracy had almost forgotten about the recent embarrassing occasion when she had gone round drunk to David's house, and was oblivious to the chaos she had caused that night. She hadn't seen David since, as last week he had been out of the office most of the time, and Tracy was really missing what she viewed as the 'intrigue' between them. Now she sat in her kitchen in a pink quilted housecoat drinking copious amounts of black coffee. She had already drunk about a litre of the stuff and still felt thirsty. She had found some lager in the fridge and wondered if drinking a couple of cans of that would be a good idea on the 'hair of the dog' principle, but decided against it. There was no point in making inroads to her own supplies when in a couple of hours' time she would be able to drink as much as she liked at someone else's expense. Her morning of trying on clothes was punctuated by frequent visits to the bathroom.

Ursula had woken up feeling tired. She had slept badly. She was worried about a number of things, all of them connected with Quentin. Would he get disgustingly drunk? (He probably would, regardless of the circumstances). Would he go off with Natasha? Although at least she would be able to get a look at Natasha for herself; no matter how gorgeous Natasha might be Ursula felt that she could better manage any threat that she posed by knowing the quality of the competition. Would Quentin make declarations of love to Simon? Knowing his form neither she nor Kate were particularly impressed by Quentin's protestations that he no longer had romantic feelings for Simon. Would the whole thing end in another relapse? Out of all the revellers-to-be Ursula was probably the only one who wished she wasn't going.

Jack, Chloe and Naomi were all really excited. Naomi had stayed over, and by eight thirty in the morning the three of them were chattering nineteen to the dozen in Chloe's bedroom, projecting. The decided who they thought would get drunk, who would end up kissing who, who would be fun, who would be boring, who would be wearing ridiculous clothes. They fully intended to drink alcohol, and were making bets with each other about this. Naomi had already tasted alcohol, though the twins hadn't. All the previous animosity between Jack and the girls seemed to have evaporated. Susan wasn't mentioned.

Joe and Mikey had a late breakfast and wandered down to the Sceptre. They had arranged to drop in after Mikey had finished helping with setting things up but before going to the party, to have a coffee with Piety, Dainty and Amos. This was mainly for Amos's benefit, because it had been decided to open the pub for a limited time, and Amos would be left to manage with Mikey and Joe to help him whilst the girls went on to the party.

Joe was tired. School classes for 'A' level students had been suspended for a couple of weeks now, since the various courses had been completed, and Joe was studying night and day. He had already done two of his exam papers, and they seemed to go quite well, but there were still seven more to go. He was so preoccupied that he didn't expect to enjoy the party much, but he knew Mikey was right when he said it would do him good to get out for a few hours.

Chapter 37

The section of Cannon Street closest to The Grange had been laid out like an open plan living area. At either end of this section a television had been set up, over each of which a makeshift canopy had been erected to protect it from the sun, although there wasn't too much of that so far. A semicircle of chairs had been arranged in front of each television set, and Piety, Quentin, Wendy and Imogen were seated together on some of these watching the familiar and not unpleasing anachronism of the royal family proceeding along The Mall in their horse drawn vehicles, while at the sides of the street cheering crowds waved little union jacks by the thousand. The party hadn't got going so far as it was still early and, predictably, most of the guests were starting out at The Sceptre. The viewers, having nothing else to do, were glued to the screen as if it were the first Martian interview.

"This has got a lot more class than Carnival," said Piety, "but it's nothing like as much fun."

Quentin gave her a pained look. "I don't see how you can compare the two."

It had been decided to arrange things semi-formally in terms of eating and drinking so that everyone could chill out in the way that suited him best, and so four trestle tables had been placed together end to end with forty or fifty chairs around them. People could choose to sit down and eat a proper meal once the main food had been brought out, or snack intermittently, buffet style, as they continued to wander around socialising. Kate had somehow contrived to fashion a snowy tablecloth out of several packets of white crepe paper. People had expressed doubts about the practicality of white, but the floral display provided by Sid looked magnificent against it. As a precaution against the possibility of rain alternative, slightly ramshackle dining arrangements had been made available in a marquee in the Dawsons' back garden. A selection of preliminary fare, with plenty of soft drinks but limited alcohol had already been set out by Dainty and Kathleen in both locations. The television watchers called Kathleen over when there was some action she might particularly want to see, but at this stage this was sparse.

Jack, Chloe, Naomi and Susan, together with a few other local kids, were drifting between one food source and the other, stuffing themselves with peanuts, crisps and drinks. The presence of other children had relaxed the potential tension between Susan, Naomi and the twins. Any hostilities among them seemed to have been suspended. Susan's confidence was increasing daily, largely as a result of what was happening in her family life, and she had even begun to suspect that Jack was at least as much on her side as he was on the others'. Now sporting their party attire David, Sid and Shane were kicking a football around further down the street, away from the party area. Mikey, Joe and

Amos were still serving at the pub, and David was now deciding that perhaps his world might not be coming to an end after all.

Kate, reluctant to go out and face the world, was hiding in the kitchen, dragging out last minute jobs that couldn't have been done any earlier. She knew that because of the commotion on that dreadful evening people would know that all was not well in the Dawson household, and she felt defensive and defiant about what they might be thinking. People's imaginations might make things out to be even worse than they were, and she had told Dainty that she was now nervous of meeting everybody.

"Bluff it out," Dainty had said, "It's none of their business. In any case most of them aren't half as interested as you imagine they are. They've all got agendas of their own, and they're much more interested in theirs than in yours, believe me," but Kate didn't have the tough mentality of the Tobagonian girls. Also, although she had taken on board everything Dainty had said about her marriage, moving on and the like, she had still hardly spoken to David and was apprehensive of coming across him whilst there were still so few people about, not to mention so much sobriety. She was hoping that later on the general inebriation and atmosphere of celebration would help them break the ice. She wondered if a splash of alcohol would help bolster her courage, and poured herself a glass of red wine. A few minutes later she was just chopping a couple of peppers for the rice salad and a cucumber for the raita when Joe, Amos and Mikey put their heads round the kitchen door.

"Anything we can do?"

Kate jumped. "Gracious! I didn't hear you coming!"

Mikey put his arms round Kate and gave her a big hug. He knew that she felt bad. He noticed the almost empty wine glass.

"Tut, tut, Kate! On the old plonk already? You need to watch that, you know."

"I know. I just fancied it this morning somehow, and after all it is getting on for twelve."

"Quite right," said Mikey, picking up the wine bottle and filling her glass up again. "This is a party. Have some more. Tracy and Tulip are outside, by the way. They've already found some vodka and started on that, and are at this very moment persuading others to do the same, so you're in good company."

"Really? Perhaps I'll come out now."

At the mention of Tracy's name Kate downed the newly poured glass of wine in one to calm the sudden churning of her stomach. In their emotional and distracted state it hadn't occurred to either her or David to ensure that Tracy didn't come, and Kate was suddenly smitten by an urgent need to engage with her instantly in an effort to smother her own fear and resentment. The effect of the wine suddenly kicked in, so that as she stepped into the outside air she felt quite unsteady. She tripped and had to grab Mikey's arm to steady herself. But now, mildly anaesthetised, she was able to say calmly and apparently cheerfully,

"You must be Tracy and Tulip. How nice to meet you. I see you've already got drinks ..."

"Yes, thanks," said Tracy. She looked Kate over carefully, including at her feet and, comparing Kate's sensible sandals with her own trendy, albeit unwieldy, platforms Tracy mentally dismissed her as dowdy.

Kate, suddenly felt, in spite of the wine, or maybe because of it, an overwhelming urge to do something really violent to Tracy, and was wondering just how violent she could get away with being without getting prosecuted. She said,

"Do help yourselves to peanuts and things. Lunch will be served in about an hour."

"Thank you," said Tulip, and smiled.

"Thanks," said Tracy, "but I'll stick with the vodka if that's okay."

"Fine. I don't know how many people here you know..."

"Just Mikey and Wendy I think," replied Tulip, "oh, and Joe. Tracy and I have both been to Mikey' salon a couple of times, but I don't think we know anyone else. I don't anyhow."

"Let me introduce you to Quentin," said Kate, but as she turned her head to see where he might be her heart almost stopped as she saw Simon climbing out of a taxi at the Ashley Road end of the street, and Quentin strolling towards him. Kate had been so engrossed recently in her own relationship problems that they had supplanted what had previously been her overriding preoccupation, the problem of Quentin – and Simon. Her intention for weeks had been above all to have a sound strategy for monitoring them both at the street party so that any impending disaster could be averted, and had then completely forgotten that Simon even existed. She would have formulated a cast iron strategy for any threatening situation that might unfold, but was now left with none at all. She could only let the situation play out as it might.

As Quentin and Kate from their different vantage points watched Simon emerging from the taxi they were surprised to see three women get out after him. They both immediately recognised Natasha, and the delight Quentin felt at seeing her totally obliterated the unpleasant, unidentifiable emotion which had hit him hard when he had seen Simon and started walking towards him. He had known Natasha was coming of course, but suddenly and unexpectedly seeing her in the flesh so that he could actually feel her aura eclipsed Simon totally, leaving Quentin with a sense of peace and invulnerability and with the confident anticipation of an idyllic day. Kate too felt immeasurably better at the sight of Natasha, which dispelled the anxiety she had felt when she saw Quentin quicken his step toward Simon. She knew that Natasha was a powerful antidote, and then wonderfully, marvellously the third person to emerge was dear Ursula. The unidentified other woman was another matter, but as the street party slowly gathered momentum it became clear that Sheila was no threat to anyone. Simon had mentioned at some point to both Quentin and Kate that he had a sister but had never said much about her as he was fearful that it might lead to him inadvertently letting his disgrace be known, and certainly neither Kate nor Quentin had ever met her before or even seen a picture of her. Both of them had assumed that they were one of those pairs of siblings who never saw one another for whatever reason. Both of them now assumed, correctly, that the four had met up at the railway station.

"Hello, Simon," cooed Quentin, suddenly cool and totally in control as he came into speaking distance of the new arrivals. "How lovely to see you." He had the feeling of Simon being on the other side of a sheet of glass. He then eased himself past Simon as casually as he could in order to embrace Natasha.

"Natasha, how wonderful that you've arrived! It quite lifts my spirits. We all so enjoyed your stay, in spite of Kate being so apprehensive before you came. She seemed to think your mother had never approved of her."

"I think it was quite difficult for Kate way back, but my mother's social prejudices have more to do with insecurity than snobbery. For myself I'm thrilled to have met Kate, and I'm so looking forward to this party!"

The volume of conversation had suddenly, in both senses of the word, begun to rise. The Sceptre had only opened at ten o'clock, but by eleven thirty Amos could see that some people were already very tipsy and needing food. He had called time, let them knock back the contents of their glasses and ushered them out, and the party area was now teeming. The preliminary supply of alcohol which had been provided for the early arrivals was exhausted and the main supply was now being opened. Mikey was the only person who registered how fast people were drinking, and others with weaker nerves might have felt apprehensive about how the day might finish up, but Mikey knew that this was what many people had come for at least as much as to celebrate Her Majesty's fifty years on the throne.

"How do you know our hosts?" Simon asked Ursula. He hadn't had the opportunity to speak to her during the brief taxi ride, as it was his sibling, who had travelled down with Natasha, whom he had been eager to chat with. Moreover he needed to speak to someone, anyone, immediately in order to neutralise the effect of such an uncomfortable sudden encounter with this poised, self-assured Quentin.

"Quentin and I have known each other for donkey's years. We overlapped at Oxford but didn't really get to know each other until much later."

"How strange that he never mentioned you."

"Well he didn't mention you to me until about three years ago, and I think at that time you had lost touch with each other."

"How's he been?"

"What did you say? It's getting awfully noisy."

"I said, 'HOW'S HE BEEN?'"

"Oh, up and down, you know what he's like."

"He seems very upbeat at the moment."

"Yes. Where's he gone? I'd like a quick pre-publication word."

"He's over there, talking to Natasha. They look very cosy I must say."

"Don't they."

Having polished off a third glass of wine Kate, to her own surprise, was beginning to enjoy herself, and even Ursula's anxiety levels had been greatly reduced by the combination of the apparently uneventful meeting between Quentin and Simon and the ingestion of a quantity of gin and tonic. She was further reassured by seeing that Quentin did not give the appearance of wanting to monopolise Natasha, which was partly because he was confident of seeing plenty of her later when she came to study in Bristol.

David had deemed it wise to stick around with Sid and Shane, and he found he liked talking to them. He had never really had a chance before. Then when they drifted off to connect with their womenfolk he latched on to Joe and Mikey. He enjoyed talking to them too. His objective was to keep occupied and be seen to be occupied, preferably with other men or the children, in other words anyone who wasn't going to make the situation between him and Kate worse, until the opportunity for approaching her and talking to her in a natural way presented itself. This particularly applied once Tracy put in an appearance. However Tracy seemed to be making no attempt to get anywhere near him, let alone talk to him. He wondered if this was out of embarrassment or because she had simply lost interest or forgotten what had happened. He suspected that it was the latter. In fact he couldn't believe that she would have come at all if she had the slightest memory of what had passed between them a few days ago. Over the last hour or so she had fawned in turn, increasingly drunk, over Mikey, Amos, Joe, Sid, Shane and

Quentin. Dainty had been on guard, drinking only fruit juice and watching her from a distance, ready to intervene at any sign of trouble. Then as Kate and Kathleen, helped by Natasha, Sheila, Imogen and Susan started bringing out plates, cutlery, glasses and baskets of rolls Dainty breathed a sigh of relief at the thought that now people, including Tracy, would slow down their drinking and start eating.

Chapter 38

"Have you seen Chloe?" asked Jack.

"She's with Naomi," said Susan. "They're out in the back garden with the rabbits. I think they're both drunk."

"Oh, no," said Jack. "Mum and Dad'll be livid. We'd better go and see. They might go and let the rabbits out, or feed them something poisonous by accident or something."

Sid found himself standing next to Piety. "What are you going to call the baby?" he asked.

"Pitcher if it's a boy, Peppermint if it's a girl."

"Wendy's expecting too," Sid ventured bashfully. He could scarcely believe the words himself.

"You kiddin'?"

"No, I'm serious."

"Wow! Cool. What you callin' yours?"

"I want to name one of my hybrids after ours, so I really hope it's a girl. If it's a girl we're going to call her Amanda. Wendy wants to name it after me if it's a boy, but I can't imagine a rose called Sidney, although I suppose there's a first time for everything. Are you going to get married soon?"

"Nope. Going to have the baby christened though."

"Supposing the pastor won't do it, the baby being illegitimate and all?"

"Illegitimate? That's the second time I heard that word in less than twenty-four hours."

"A baby needs a father and a mother."

"It's got a father an' a mother, they just ain't getting married to each other, that's all. What's the problem? The minister can't refuse to baptise a person jus' 'cos their parents ain't married, can he? Anyways, s' posing the mother don't even know who the father is, for goodness sake? Is that the baby's fault?"

"I love your dress," said Susan.
"Thank you!" said Wendy.
"You look pretty cool altogether," said Susan. "Your skin looks amazing."
Bless the child, thought Wendy, she's really very sweet. I misjudged her. I wonder if I could get her to baby sit later on.

"Where's Chloe?" asked Kate.
"I don't know," said Jack.
"She's being sick in the bathroom," said Wendy.
"Damn," said Kate. "Has she been drinking?"
"She and Naomi have been knocking it back a bit," said Imogen.
"Oh, well, it's too late now. I'll speak to Chloe tomorrow. Where's Naomi?"
"Asleep on the back terrace," said Susan. Unusually for her she hadn't taken advantage of the day's exceptional circumstances to get drunk herself.

"Hells bells, her parents will be here soon. "What on earth shall I tell them?"

"The thing is," said Tulip, "it looks as though I could be in line for a major promotion at work in a couple of years or so, and I'm feeling really torn. My folks back in Jamaica would be so proud of me, they are already of course, but part of me feels that for their sake maybe I should stay here and carry on in the same job until then, and take the promotion if I get it. But the other half of me desperately wants to go back home, at least for a while. I miss my brothers and sisters, I miss the beach ..."

"And the reggae," suggested Sheila

"Well, I don't know so much about that. There's plenty of that round here, you know, especially late on summer nights."

Here comes my brother. Hello Simon, this is Tulip, a colleague of David's. Tulip, meet my brother Simon, he's a painter."

"Of pictures? How wonderful. What do you paint?"

"Mostly landscapes, some portraits, still life occasionally."

"What do you paint in?"

255

"Mostly oils, which are considered passé by some people, but so far I haven't been able to get on with acrylics, and people who use those use them for different painting styles. For example the Impressionists might have liked them if they'd been available but it's unlikely that the Old Masters could even have used them at all. I'd like to paint in a tropical setting where colour is brasher, more vibrant because of the light, but not somewhere as remote as the South Sea Islands."

"Well if the Caribbean would do maybe my family could put you up."

There was a pause. Then Simon said,

"*Seriously?*"

"As someone known to me they would almost certainly let you have a really nice room for a peppercorn rent. They've got the space. Come and sit down at the table and I'll draw you a map of Jamaica."

"Could you get me another orange juice, please?" asked Imogen.

"Good girl," said Shane, taking her glass.

"Why don't you want to go to Oxford? I thought everyone wanted to go to Oxford."

"Do you?"

"Well, not particularly, but I'm not that kind of person."

"What makes you think that I am?"

"Sorry. Actually I haven't absolutely decided that I will go to university anyway."

"I was one of those. I haven't played at all since I've been with Imogen, but I didn't have the education that you are embarking on, and I definitely believed that if I kept trying I could get to the top. We should have a game some time when you've finished your exams."

"I've only just heard your news. Congratulations."

"Thanks, Imogen. You too."

"Thanks. Ours was a bit of a surprise, but Shane's over the moon."

"So's ours, and so's Sid."

"I like your shoes (hic). Nice jacket too. I work with David (hic). You live in Cannon Street?"

"No. I'm a friend of Joe's. I live Muller Road way."

"Aren't they having a street party?"

"Well, yeah, but I've just popped down here for a bit to see Joe and a couple of other people I know."

"That your girlfriend (hic)?"

"Who?"

"The blonde girl you're staring at?"

"No. Probably never will be."

"Really? Would you like her to be? Maybe I'll go and talk to her (hic)."

"More salad Sis? That baby needs its vitamins."

"What?"

"I said "'MORE SALAD?'"

"Oh, yes please. No cucumber, plenty tomato and heavy on the mayonnaise. Oh, and lots of pickle."

"Have you spoken to Kate yet?"

"Briefly. She asked me to keep an eye on Naomi and the twins' drinking. Her demeanour was neutral. I had to put Chloe to bed. How about you and Simon?"

"He arrived with Natasha, his sister Sheila and Ursula, whom he met by chance at the station. I only had a chance to greet them briefly before being engulfed by two women from your office. One of them is now appallingly drunk."

"That would be Tracy."

"Aha. What a lucky escape you have had."

"What are you doing out of bed? Are you feeling better?"

"Yes. Can I have something to eat? I'm starving."

"Check with your mother, and take it easy."

"I see Ellen's talking to Alan. Why isn't she talking to you?"

"We have been talking."

"What about?"

"Conservation and the environment."

"I despair of you. You're going to die a lonely old man."

"By the way, Dainty, who's that pretty little blonde?"

"That's a friend of Joe's. I don't know the lad she's talking to, probably another friend of Joe's. But you haven't said how it's actually going with David."

"I haven't had a chance to find out. It's fairly non-committal at the moment. The only thing we've talked about today is the children's drinking. David's been doing front of house really well, looking after the young, the old and the pregnant, I'm almost in love with him again, and it's nice that he's been getting to know Simon and Sheila. He's a bit subdued, I feel a bit sorry for him. Perhaps I should give him a chance. I'm not seeing things quite so dramatically now. Given all the circumstances I think I may have overreacted. Maybe we've both been rather immature."

"Good for you."

"Have you seen Mikey?"

"Yes, he and Amos have gone to get their instruments and we're going to have some music."

"Fantastic."

"If you two could liaise and do something imaginative with our garden that would be brilliant, and it would give our B and B project a boost once we get it started. No favours, we'll pay the going rate."

"I'm up for that. It would be nice to have a project I could get really stuck into and not just do weeding and mowing lawns most of the time."

"Me too, it would be great to grow more and bigger plants even though they wouldn't be for me or my own little garden."

"Sorted yourself out with those Dawson kids have you?"

"Yes, it's fine now. I've said I'm sorry and they're not angry."

"Good for you. Young Jack's going to have a try out for our choir. Give him summat to do while his sister's off dancing. Why don't you come along too?"

"How's it going, old thing?"

"Well, David and I have hardly spoken, but most likely it's because we've both been really busy with other people, and he and that dreadful woman haven't been anywhere near each other. Now that I've come across her I realise that she's no threat whatsoever, I just can't understand what David was doing with her in the first place. It might have been because he wasn't happy and I hadn't noticed, and maybe he didn't fully realise either, and she was just ready to slot herself in. But at the very least I'm ready to discuss it with him now. This party's been an absolute boon, the only thing that's got me through the day. I'm really enjoying it, but tomorrow will be such an anti-climax I just don't know if I'll be able to handle it. How about you and Quentin?"

"We haven't spoken much either. Quite honestly we don't seem to have much to talk about. Still, he seems quite unperturbed, which is the main thing."

"I hear you are going to have a little sibling."

"What's a sibling?"

"A brother or sister."

"Oh, yes, I'm hoping for a sister. I can help her with her fashion choices."

"Hmm."

"I used to have a riding school, but now I'm hoping to start a career in interior design."

"Really? Kate's about to start up in interior design as well."

"Yes," said Kate, "I think I've managed to squeeze onto a course at the Technical College here."

"No! I'm starting there in September too. How amazing that we're both going to do interior design. We really must keep in touch until then."

"Of course we will. I think we can rely on Natasha to see to that! Gracious, look at the time! And the hot food's coming out! Where's my gong?"

Chapter 39

Appetites had been well sharpened by the alcohol, and by the time Kate's third gong stroke had died away people were converging on the central table.

"Hurry, everyone," yelled Piety, "Come an' get it while it's hot!"

Life can turn on a sixpence they say. It can also turn on a seating arrangement, random or contrived. David had decided that he was going to make sure that he sat next to Kate. They would be forced to be nice to each other in front of other people whether they felt like it or not, and then by the time the meal was over even if they weren't the best of friends at least they would have regained the habit of talking to each other again. The fact that Ursula and Quentin were together was intentional on both their parts. Joe had made a point of grabbing a seat next to an unsuspecting Natasha (to the satisfaction of both Quentin and Ursula), whilst since Tracy and Alan were not only seated well before everyone else got to the table but also kissing passionately, it could be taken that theirs was a mutual decision. Alan had become increasingly drunk and more desolate as he came to realise that Ellen had no romantic aspirations where he was concerned, and Tracy's own inebriation lent itself to her predatory prowess. Some had no preference and sat down wherever there was room. Shane and Imogen and Sid and Wendy stayed with their partners. Sheila found herself next to Mikey, and Simon and Tulip remained together, still engrossed in the drawing of Jamaica on the tablecloth. The many children present sat in groups, partly random, partly according to choice. Chloe and Naomi, now remarkably recovered, sat together and so did Jack and Susan.

All in all the day was a success, although anticlimactic for some after the recent drama at The Grange, which was perhaps no bad thing. The majority of the participants, now well-fed and watered, were clearly enjoying themselves and most were fairly drunk. David's tactics proved effective – more so than he could have realised from Kate's conversation and behaviour before and during the meal. She drank in a restrained way, he hardly at all. She was polite but remote. He was charm personified. It was as though through months of rubbing shoulders with Quentin on a daily basis something of Quentin's charisma was informing David's own personality. Kate was feeling strangely shy, and David was seeing next to him the Kate he had first met all those years ago. It helped that they had each noticed Tracy and Alan wrapped round one another, which distanced both David and Kate's feelings from the recent unpleasant events once and for all. Between the main course and the dessert, when Kate went to get up to help clear the former away, Kathleen whispered conspiratorially in her ear, "Stay where you are, dear, you've done quite enough already," and whisked the dirty dishes out of her hands.

With people constantly getting up from their seats and going to sit somewhere else, Quentin and Ursula found themselves sitting opposite Joe and Natasha, and were soon enfolded in the tranquil companionability of the two young people. Slowly absorbing their mood of happy anticipation of the future gave Ursula an extraordinary sense of weightlessness, although the alcohol could have had something to do with this, and Quentin began to feel the cares of the world sliding from his shoulders. His earlier tension had dissipated and been replaced by a sense of deep serenity, largely due to the goddess sitting opposite him. It felt like an inoculation, as though he had been rendered immune to the angst of many years. Quentin knew for certain that he had negotiated an important corner, whether under his own impetus or by the force of circumstances he didn't know, nor could he tell whether it had been a process or had just suddenly happened, and in the privacy of his own head he was examining the situation. It was now obvious that it was Sheila who had answered the phone to him all those weeks ago. Quentin had found that he really liked Sheila for herself and not only because she was Simon's sister rather than his girlfriend, and this gave him a pleasure which was stronger than any residual feeling he might have for Simon. It was remarkable how everything seemed to be falling into place. Moreover Ursula, the person he most trusted in the world, not just from a professional point of view but also a personal one, given Kate's own tendency to neurosis, was seated at his right hand. Natasha, who was as much the most beautiful girl in the world as Simon was the most beautiful boy, and who still had the youthfulness that was beginning to fade in Simon, sat smiling at him from across the table. Young Joe had his arm around her shoulders, which struck Quentin as completely appropriate, a feeling which confirmed to him that he didn't actually want Natasha for himself. As he sat there absorbing all this Quentin wished that everything could stay exactly the same as it was now for the rest of his life.

Joe was sublimely happy. He had found his true love, even though she might not realise it yet. His thoughts drifted to Ellen. She and Becky were chatting happily further down the table. He had always realised that Alan wasn't right for her, and knew that she had some exciting gap year plans which could be compromised if she was in a serious relationship. Inwardly he grinned at the idea of Tracy being Alan's first experience with a woman, nevertheless it wouldn't necessarily be one without its merits.

Pots of tea and cafetières of coffee were now being put on the table. Tracy and Alan had disappeared, though nobody except Kate and David had noticed this. Most of the children had gone off to find something more interesting to do. Some of them had gone into the Dawsons' back garden and were trying to play a game of cricket, which proved difficult to sustain because of the length of the grass. Chloe and Naomi had gone up to Chloe's bedroom. Jack and

Susan were sitting together looking at a gardening book with Sid and Wendy.

After some more shuffling around and regrouping of the guests Simon and Tulip, still poring over the map upon which Tulip sporadically wrote or drew something, now found themselves seated opposite Mikey and Sheila, who had come up to join them.

"Obviously Jamaica's the island I know best," said Tulip, but I've got friends In Barbados and also in the Leeward Islands, so you wouldn't be limited to just one island."

"And I've got family in Trinidad," offered Mikey. "If it's people and action you want try Port of Spain, the capital, although you increasingly need to watch out for the violence which, sadly, is a growing problem, but Tobago, its sister island, is quieter and really beautiful."

The alcohol began to flow once more, and Ursula pounced on it eagerly. None of her terrible fears had come to pass over the last few hours but the strain of vigilance, together with the substantial amounts of gin that she had already consumed, was beginning to tell. She felt she and Kate had got Quentin through thus far, and rather felt that the rest was up to him. Quentin, following her lead, cautiously picked up a glass of wine and took a couple of sips.

An hour later Natasha and Joe excused themselves and it surprised both Simon and Quentin, being the only relatively sober people among the six remaining at the table, to realise suddenly that most of the other partiers were now dancing to deafening rock music some way down the street, where one television set had been disconnected to make way for a sound system. Some of them wandered down to have a look, but Simon had a sudden urge to leave. He briefly wondered whether he should wait for his sister, but since she was staying overnight at The Grange, whereas he had a room booked in the centre of town, there was not much point in him waiting. Sheila would be quite safe, drunk as she was, in the present company, and he could say goodbye to her in the morning.

It was with the merest twinge that Quentin watched him go.

Chapter 40

"These are the two youngsters I told you about," said Sid. "Perhaps you could arrange with them about when they could come for a try-out."

Dick, the choirmaster, beamed at Jack and Susan.

"We'll have a go now," he said. "No time like the present. Where do your families worship? I don't recall seeing either of you before."

"They don't," said Jack.

"Mine neither," said Susan. "They'll think I'm really barmy when they find out I'm in a church choir. If you let me in, that is," she added hastily. "They think religious people are weird, although Shane does yoga."

Dick laughed. "We won't worry about that. Let's go over to the piano."

An hour and a half later Jack and Susan left the church hall and made off towards Jack's house feeling very pleased with themselves. Dick had said that their singing was good enough for both of them to be in the church choir, and they would begin attending choir practice in the autumn, on Friday evenings.

A lot had changed for both children. David had been spending more time with Jack. They had been going to watch cricket every week since the season began, and David had just enrolled them both for some cricket coaching. Jack no longer felt eclipsed or controlled by his sister, and although he sometimes missed her now that they were growing apart in some ways, he was no longer dependent on her, and they were still very connected with each other. Sid, too, had helped Jack find his feet.

During the half term holiday Kate had invited Susan to lunch while her mother went to a hospital appointment. It was hard to believe that a few months previously she had been watching the Dawsons from the overgrown path, desperately wanting to become acquainted with them. A few weeks ago it had seemed that she belonged nowhere, and now she belonged in two places, for of course she now also belonged in a family of her own. For the first time in her life she had two parents, and was going to have a baby brother or sister.

The pair of them ran down the street together, laughing.

Chapter 41

"All's well that ends well, then," said Dainty. She had been coming round every morning to help Kate get straight after the party.

"Mmm," said Kate. She sat gazing through the open window and over the back garden, where David was mowing the lawn. You could actually see that there was a lawn now. David had promised new flower beds, and Sid had offered his surplus bedding plants. Kate was contentedly anticipating a riot of colour in the garden later in the summer.

Once the garden was in some kind of order David was going to help Kate finish the inside of the house – or at the very minimum the two currently unused bedrooms, as their idea of taking in lodgers was possibly going to materialise earlier than expected as they knew that both Sheila and Natasha would want accommodation for the coming Autumn. David had made a lot of concessions lately, and Kate had agreed that he was right in saying that large houses were for large numbers of people, and that she didn't need a sewing room as such any more than the twins needed a games room, and the sooner they rented the rooms out the better. Her liking for both Natasha and Sheila had made it easy for Kate to concede on this issue, hoping as she did that these two would be their first lodgers. Moreover in spite of her late application she had been accepted on the same interior design course as Sheila, which was hugely exciting. What with a new career looming and a new romance with her own husband Kate's cup was full, and these things were promising to fill the gap that was growing as the twins became less dependent on her in practical areas.

Chloe had been offered, and with the blessing of her parents accepted, a place at the Curzon Academy of ballet. She was spending more and more time with Naomi, who was also starting at the Academy. They were becoming increasingly girly, with ear piercings and nail polish. The difficulties between Chloe and Jack had been resolved of course, but it still gave Kate a twinge to notice that they didn't seem as close as they once were. Not only was Jack spending more time both with his father and with Susan but he was also becoming a different boy. He was singing in the church with Sid and Susan and spending time in the cricket nets with his Dad, as well as helping in the garden. He was brimful of energy and ideas.

"More juice?"

"No thanks. I've got a bit of acidity this morning. Have you got a glass of cold milk?"

"Of course." Getting up to go and fetch it Kate looked sideways at her friend, then looked again. She had never seen her looking so relaxed and dreamy. Then the penny dropped.

"Oh, Dainty ... you're not ... you *can't* be, *surely* not you too?"

Dainty grinned broadly.

"Here's hoping, but don't get too excited, I'm not sure yet. I'm going to buy one of those test kits this afternoon."

"Well I hope so too. That would be wonderful. A cousin for Pitcher or Peppermint. Speaking of which, how is Piety?"

"She's acting strange."

"She's pregnant. She's allowed to."

"But she's out all the time, mostly late at night. She comes home at all hours. I bumped into Mikey yesterday grinning all over his face. "When's the wedding?" he said. I said, "What wedding?" and he just laughed and walked on. It's not like him to be mysterious, and I wondered if he was referring to Piety, but she ain't said nuttin' to us, and it's a waste of time axin' her questions."

"She always insists that she doesn't want to get married."

"Exactly. I just don't know what's going on."

"Well, all you can do is wait and see what happens. It seems that you have plenty in your own life to see to without worrying about everyone else."

Chapter 42

"You're not still doing that same bit of floor are you?" asked Ursula impatiently. "You need to get a move on or this is going to take for ever."

"It's all very well for you," replied Quentin petulantly. "You're used to it. You're a girl from humble beginnings. Of course you know how to hang curtains and get traces of concrete off parquet flooring. I, on the other hand, did not grow up with your advantages."

He dragged his bare wrist – it was too warm a day for him to have an actual cuff available – across his nostrils to catch the drip that was forming there. He then wiped his wrist on his expensive new jeans. He had never even owned a pair of jeans before, and he was wearing these for the first time and finding them uncomfortable. If he had bothered to ask anybody they could have told him that cheaper jeans are usually more comfortable than more expensive ones because they are made of thinner material.

"Well, whatever isn't finished this week you're going to have to do without me. I'm not giving up any more of my annual leave to help you clean up your wretched house."

Ursula was as much in love with Quentin as ever, and she as much as anyone wanted to see him move into his new house, but she was discovering that relationships, especially the kind about which she had been dangerously fantasising, are always more tricky than anticipated.

"You're all façade," she continued unkindly. "I bet all those high and mighty colleagues of yours, who are so impressed by your academic ability and knowledge and also maybe, I grudgingly admit, by your style and wit, would be quite appalled at your total ineptitude when it comes to a bit of domestic planning and cleaning up."

"That's only because most of them have got wives and have no idea how difficult such things are. They wouldn't be able to do them either."

However in spite of her irritation at Quentin's inadequacies Ursula was delighted that he was taking so much interest in the house. The emotional exhaustion that had overtaken him earlier in the year had proved terminal for his relationship with Simon, although of course there had been other factors involved in this as well. During the street party he had surreptitiously scrutinised his friend and noticed how much older he was looking. His features were changing and becoming coarser. The sartorial indifference, however, which had seemed rather charming years ago, had not changed at all, and Quentin had thought Simon looked rather scruffy, and not in a good way, particularly next to Natasha. Natasha had a perfect figure, a perfect complexion, an impeccable taste in clothes and a bank balance to be able to indulge it. She had a better personality than Simon had ever had. She had recently adopted the gamine hairstyle already sported by Chloe and Susan, which gave her such a deliciously androgynous look that it made the hairs on the back of Quentin's neck stand on end.

"If you can't get what you want, want what you get," Quentin's grandmother had been fond of saying. Maybe she was right. Quentin looked back over the last few weeks: time spent with Ursula – finishing his paper, working on the house, in restaurants, at the theatre; time spent with Kate and the twins; time spent meeting new people – Natasha, Sheila, Tulip, Cannon Street folk. These things had come his way without much effort on his part. Did he want them? Definitely. Then he looked at the years that had passed since Simon first went to Dorset. These had been times of angst, paranoia, irrational, unpredictable behaviour and frustration which drove his friends to despair. Did he want them back? Definitely not. The street party had told him all he needed to know – what Kate and Ursula had been telling him all along. Simon wasn't interested. And now he didn't want a relationship with Simon either. The madness had passed.

A year or two ago Quentin had wanted to finish the house as quickly as his ailing health would allow, since obviously the sooner he finished it the sooner Simon would be able to move in, but the more despairing he became about his relationship with Simon the less keen he became to finish it, because to finish the house was to have everyone expect him to move into it permanently, by himself. Now, however, what with Natasha coming to live in Bristol and the increasing regularity with which he was spending time with Ursula, and most importantly the releasing of Simon's grip on him emotionally, he felt much more upbeat about life and interested in making changes, but he still had a hesitancy when it came to actually moving into The Studio. For all his posing and attempts at faking an aloof and self-sufficient persona he didn't actually like being alone.

Then the idea struck. The house was spacious, in fact by normal standards far too large to be occupied by one person. In view of this, maybe it would be a good idea to invite Ursula to come and share it with him, as a lodger. She didn't earn that much by London standards, and her East Croydon two bedroomed flat was undeniably dreary. They had a lot in common, particularly work and friends, and there was easily enough space for them to have guests together or individually and still not be on top of one another. Quentin was astounded that he hadn't thought of this before, and it didn't occur to him that Ursula might not accept. He was so excited that he wanted to put it to her straight away, but decided more prudently to wine and dine her at the weekend at a top restaurant and put it to her then.

Chapter 43

"Hi." Tulip poked her head round the door of David's office.

He looked up and smiled. "Come in, Tulip."

She sank back into an easy chair. "What did you want to see me about?"

By way of reply he handed her a letter bearing yesterday's date. It was dated the thirty-first of July.

Dear David,

It is with great pleasure that I am writing to you to tender my resignation. I shall be leaving work at the end of August. To be exact my last day at work will be 31/08/02.

I am getting married to my fiancé, Alan Preston, on October 27th 2002. We are expecting a baby on March 31st 2003.

Please accept my best wishes for your future plans.

Yours sincerely,

Tracy Unwin.

Tulip looked up and saw that David was grinning broadly. "Not a lot you can say really."

"Except that she doesn't let the grass grow under her feet. That boy's father's worth a bob or two. He makes a fortune with his building business. I wonder what he'll have to say about this. If Daddy doesn't take to her she could be on a hiding to nowhere and lumbered with that chinless wonder for nothing."

"You're forgetting about the baby."

"That's true. Oh well, I suppose you've got to hand it to her."

"Actually, David, I'm glad you called me in because there's something else I need to talk to you about."

"Oh?" David felt a little uneasy.

"Well, it's not imminent, but I felt it only fair, in the circumstances, to let you know as far in advance as possible."

"Spit it out, Tulip."

"Well, you know we were talking a little while ago about me applying for your job in two or three years' time?"

"Well?"

"I won't be applying for it. I won't be here."

"Really? Then where the hell will you be?"

"Jamaica."

"Oh. I have heard whispers that you had begun to feel homesick."

"I have."

"When are you planning to go?"

"Early in the New Year."

"Tulip, couldn't you leave it a bit longer? Are you really going to let me struggle on without you in this ghastly department for my last year or two? Come on, now!"

"Well, the thing is, it's not entirely down to me."

"Really? Who else is it down to?"

Tulip hesitated. "Simon."

"Simon? Simon who?"

"Simon Barnes."

"Quentin's Simon? You're kidding."

"I'm not. He's told me all about his relationship with Quentin. He knows he was using him and eventually realised he had to stop. But now that his painting is taking a new direction, in the sense that he wants to work in an entirely different culture where strong colours and natural lighting are more prominent – he says he's looking for something more vibrant visually and wants to experiment in a tropical location."

"Like Gauguin?"

"Just like Gauguin."

"Where do you fit in?"

Tulip hesitated again. "Well, I have family out there that I could introduce him to. Now that Quentin is out of his life, and let's face it, now that Quentin's money is out of his life, Simon's got to look elsewhere, to put it crudely, for the wherewithal of survival. He has a little money of his own, not much, but if he could stay with my family for a while, just for long enough to find out if this change of artistic direction is going to pay off financially, it might give him a chance of carrying on with his painting. If it didn't work he could give it all up and go into teaching, satisfied that at least he had given it his best shot."

"You don't think he could be about to use you in the same way he used Quentin?"

"It's possible. But you've got to admit that Quentin and I are two very different people. The minute I don't feel comfortable about Simon he'll be out of the door."

"Of course there's nothing romantic going on among all this, is there?"

Tulip flashed him her brightest smile.

"See you in the morning David," she said, and left the room.

Chapter 44

"A pint of bitter for me and tomato juice for the young lady. Lots of Worcester sauce."

"She'll look like a tomato if she carries on like this," said Amos.

Imogen smiled. Amos fancied her more every day. "I seem to be addicted to it."

"Don't worry, love. You won't want to know it once the baby's born. Where's the young 'un today?"

"Off somewhere with Jack Dawson. Thick as thieves they are now. Where's Piety?"

"Restin'. It's startin' to get on top of her. She's only just over seven months and bigger than an elephant. She actin' strange too. Goes out a lot more than she ought to if you axe me. No wonder she's tired. Looks like we're goin' to have to manage without her over the rest of the summer just when it's gettin' really busy."

"Shane'll give you a hand, won't you, love?" Imogen had mellowed out no end during the last few weeks.

"He wouldn't want to leave you on your own, would he? Specially now."

"I'd like to spend time on my own with Susan a couple of evenings a week, and I go over to Wendy's on Tuesdays anyway."

Shane grinned. "What do you think, Amos?"

"Sounds great. Minimum wage, mind."

Shane laughed. "It'll pay for the buggy."

"And the champagne," said Imogen.

"What champagne?" asked Shane.

"At the wedding."

"What wedding?"

"Ours. Will you marry me?"

Shane stared at her. There was a long pause. Then he said,

"You bet!"

At this point Amos scuttled out the back as fast as his legs would carry him, so was unable to describe for Dainty and Piety the way in which Shane took Imogen in his arms and kissed her.

Chapter 45

Dear Joe,

Congratulations! Three A*'s! You must be over the moon. I bet Mikey's proud. I only got two A*s and an A, but I'm definitely coming to Bristol, so I'm really glad you're spending your gap year working and not going travelling. I'll have you to keep me company as well as Quentin, at least for as long as he's still at The Grange. And it'll give you a year to choose what you want to study. I can help you decide since I'm three months older than you and therefore wiser!

After my first year exams next June I'm planning to go to India for the rest of the summer. I want to do it the hippy way like other people but Mum is dead against it. I think Dad understands, but she says it's daft when we've got so much family over there and I could so easily stay with them. She just doesn't get it. Do you fancy coming with me? She might not be so jumpy if I wasn't going on my own. RSVP.

Love, Tash

. . . .

Dear David and Kate,

I'm glad you've finally agreed to get online! I can't understand how you've managed for so long, but I suppose the modern world gets us all in the end!

Kate, I'm finding the idea of us being on the same interior design course really exciting, and it's in that connection that I'm e-mailing you. Natasha let it slip that you may have rooms to let in your house, and since I will need to find somewhere to live, this is to enquire as to whether or not you will have any vacancies for the autumn term. I can recommend myself as a lodger on the basis that I am ten years older than the average first year student and do not come in particularly late, get drunk (well, not very and not often) or make a lot of noise.

The fallout from your wonderful street party last month is quite intoxicating. There is a steady correspondence now between Mikey and myself and also between Joe and Natasha. Isn't it deliciously incestuous!

If your reply about accommodation is in the negative, well never mind, I'll still look forward to seeing you at college!

Best wishes to you and yours,

Sheila Barnes

Chapter 46

Simon and Sheila stood and looked at the piles of paintings piled round the walls of the attic in Simon's cottage

"Maybe Kate and David could store them for you, and probably your books as well. They've got masses of space."

"I hardly think they'd want to, given their connection with Quentin."

"Oh, nonsense. Whatever makes you think that anybody cares about any relationship that you and Quentin might have had? I'm sure David and Kate don't, and in any case they gave me to understand that Quentin may move out soon."

"Well, if they could take them for the time being it would solve a major problem. I can't think of anywhere else I could leave them. Everything else here can be junked. It can either go to one of the charity shops or to the dump."

"Only after I've looked through it all to see if I want anything. I'm going to be an impoverished student, remember."

Tulip and Simon had indeed decided to go to the Caribbean together. They had been in constant touch since the street party but were giving nothing away regarding the precise nature of their relationship in spite of the speculation among their family and friends. The enormity of the change in itself for each of them was quite enough to deal with without having to give other people information regarding questions they were far from being able to answer for themselves. It can only be said that recently they had each become aware of being weighed down by a feeling of staleness, depression even, in both their personal and professional lives, so that the sudden possibility of a dramatic change of scene with the support of a likeable someone else in the same situation was highly attractive, and was filling them with optimism and excitement. Although neither of them was ready to define their relationship and felt no need to do so they each felt that thinking of the immediate future in the context of 'us' rather than 'me' was a nice feeling, and onlookers were commenting on the 'chemistry' between the two.

It was now August, and the rainy season had already begun in the Caribbean, so it was not the ideal time to go. Simon, embarrassed by the memory of the degree to which he had sponged off Quentin over the years, was determined to be self-supporting. From an ego point of view he would have liked to have been able to finance Tulip as well, but this would not be possible nor, in any case, was she likely to agree to it. They came to the conclusion that the best thing to do was to go in the New Year when the rainy season would be over and the Caribbean countryside benefitting from it, but now that change was in the air Simon was longing to get away from the cottage, his home of five years, and in particular didn't want to spend another winter in this isolated rural spot. Tulip had suggested that he come and live with her in Bath until after Christmas, as his chances of getting a temporary job there were good. In fact he quickly obtained a job to go to at the end of the month at the Bristol Old Vic as a set painter, and he was really looking forward to it. It was only a few hundred metres from where Tulip worked, so if he stayed with her in Bath she would be able to give him a lift each day. Most astonishing of all the Arnolfini Gallery in Bristol city centre was running an art exhibition and sale of new landscape painters and had selected four of Simon's pictures that it was willing to accept on a sale or return basis, although there was no guarantee that any of them would definitely be displayed. Simon was also planning to do evening bar work in Bath. In the next four and a half months he was determined to earn and put by as much money as possible.

Mikey had numerous cousins and other relatives in Trinidad who could put them up temporarily, and Tulip and Simon were planning to go there first, at the end of January, to enable them to be in Port of Spain for Carnival in Trinidad, spread over several days and in itself a great painting opportunity for Simon. He would have the chance to make action sketches of dancers, record colours, visit the costume makers and pan yards where, correspondingly, the character outfits and steel drums required for this dazzling spectacle were produced. Then the pair of them would go on to

Jamaica where Simon would paint until his money ran out. In the meantime Tulip intended to do a bit of networking with a view to deciding whether or not she wanted to move her life permanently to Jamaica or not.

Chapter 47

Miss Piety Rosemary Brown and Mr Byron Dionysus Williams

request the pleasure of your company

on the occasion of their marriage

at

Stockton Pentecostal Church

on

Saturday 31st August 2002

at 12.00 noon

Please bring your musical instruments

And afterwards at The Dugout Club

Kate immediately phoned The Sceptre.

"For heaven's sake, Dainty, that's the Saturday after next. It's not a lot of notice, is it? And surely a lot of people will be on holiday?"

"Most of Piety's friends can't afford holidays, said Dainty cheerfully, "and the ones who really matter will be there anyway. We checked. Not only that, it had to be arranged as soon as possible, while she's still able to get down the aisle. She's over eight months now and barely mobile, but she's decided that she wants the baby to be born legitimate."

"I can't believe this is Piety you're talking about."

"Me neither. Looks like she's takin' a turn for the better."

"How sad. If that's the case I'm going to miss the Piety I used to know."

"Me too, but that's progress for you."

"What happened anyway? I mean, she was adamant that she didn't want to get married."

"I know. Byron is the baby's father, as I suspected, but he's not half as sexy as his brother, Piecrust. For a couple of years Piety has been lusting after Piecrust, which is probably how she got involved with Byron in the first place. Due to the madness of infatuation she's been holding out for Piecrust in spite of the baby's actual paternity, but since she discovered that now he's got a new, gorgeous, younger-than-Piety girlfriend she's decided to cut her losses and marry Byron. She's very wise because although Byron's no oil painting he's got a good job and he'll make a great dad and a great husband. All this running around she's been doing lately, has been them secretly, so say, going out together, even up to the Dugout. All she can do there is sit and listen, but she loves the music and the atmosphere. That's why she's been coming home late, and that's why Mikey clicked on before the rest of us. Amos doesn't play the Dugout much in the summer, we're too busy. We only found out a couple of weeks ago when they needed to start having the bans read out."

"Is there a present list?"

"Just bring as much food and drink as you can."

"No problem. There's still a good deal of stuff left over from the street party sitting in my freezer."

Chapter 48

It took Amos and the driver some minutes to ease Piety out of the car without damaging her dress. She rearranged herself little by little, then moved towards the small welcoming party.

"You look radiant," said Quentin, lifting her fingers to his lips and kissing them. Piety bestowed a dazzling smile upon him and proceeded with Amos towards the church steps. Amos, upon whose arm she was leaning heavily, looked as though he might cave in under the weight.

"I agree with you," said David. "She looks lit from within. And so do you, my love," he said, turning to Kate.

"It's the light of happiness," said Kate.

The church was packed. There were guests from Trinidad and Tobago, St. Vincent and the Grenadines, St. Lucia, Manchester, Birmingham and London. Most of the rest were local. Every seat was taken apart from those in the second row which were reserved for the welcoming party. Any latecomers were going to have to stand at the back. Standing at the front, at either side of the preacher, were the musicians from the Dugout with the exception, of course, of Amos, accompanied by any number of other musicians with their instruments.

Quentin, Kate and David scurried to their seats next to the twins just as the preacher gave a pre-arranged signal to the person standing at the inner door for Piety and Amos to start their walk down the aisle. At the same time Amos winked at the band which, Caribbean style, instantly broke into a deafening rendition of 'When The Saints Go Marching In' to accompany Piety's slow and lumbering progress, and suddenly the aisles were full of frenetically dancing wedding guests, jigging and jitterbugging, twisting and twirling, feet twinkling and arms waving, all yelling along with the music, those in the centre aisle melting away by degrees back to their seats as Piety approached. The Reverend, though hoping to avoid all this shemozzle, was half expecting it, so took it in his stride.

The minute the bride stopped in front of the preacher and next to her husband-to-be all sound ceased and you could have heard a pin drop.

The preacher took a step forward, waited a full two minutes then said,

"God is love, and those who live in love live in God and God lives in them."

The silence was total. He continued,

"In the presence of God, Father, Son and Holy Spirit, we have come together to witness the marriage of Byron and Piety …,"

"Hallelujah! Praise the Lord!"

"... pray for God's blessing on them ..."

"Thank you Lord!"

"... and share their joy and celebrate their love."

"Hallelujah! Hallelujah! Hallelujah!"

The air was thick with shouts and whistles. Some people jumped up and stood on the pews, and there was much stamping of feet.

The entire service was punctuated by this rumpus.

The preacher continued patiently, pausing at times to let the hubbub subside, and eventually the binding together of Piety and Byron in holy matrimony was achieved. He had to wait a full five minutes after the exchanging of the rings while the whole place erupted, and the final song went on amid further frenzied dancing and with much repetition for twenty-five minutes.

"I've never seen anything like it," yelled Kate to Quentin at the top of her voice, but he only saw her lips move.

Back at the Dugout, which had been chosen over the Sceptre as the best venue for continuing the celebrations, it was, at first, quieter. People arrived in dribs and drabs, and were at last able to hear themselves and each other speak. The quantities of glorious food waiting to be eaten put the street party, which had been lavish, to shame. Drinks were over the bar and had to be paid for, but even so replenishments were being sent for within the first hour. For a while the music was recorded, to give the band a chance to rest, eat and drink.

When hunger and thirst had been at least partially assuaged the noise began to build up again.

"But I'll never cope with all the commuting," said Ursula.

"Oxford's not that far from London, but you can always change your job," said Quentin. "With your qualifications, experience and track record I would have thought you might get a job at the Bodleian, for example. I believe there may be a couple of vacancies coming up soon."

Quentin was finding that life was moving at a pace outside his comfort zone. Things were changing fast. Sheila and Natasha were moving into the Grange next month and although Kate had kindly said "You don't have to go, Quentin, just because of them," he knew he did. For a start it would feel too crowded. Secondly to be under the same roof as Simon's sister, and thus to be constantly informed of Simon's movements, was not to be recommended. Thirdly, to be living under the same roof as Natasha would be positively foolhardy. It also occurred to him that neither Kate nor the twins would be as available to him as they had once been, now that their lives were changing too.

Not all the changes were on the debit side, however. Quentin had found a friend in David since the crisis in the Dawson marriage. He had met and become friends with Natasha. He had come to know and like several individuals local to The Grange, where presumably he would continue to be a regular visitor. Maybe, apart from Kate and her father, these were the first real friends he had ever had. They took him as he was, and he them. They had begun to feel like family. This was a very different kettle of fish from his professional relationships, with their insincerities, one-upmanship and back stabbings. It was true that he enjoyed contact with his colleagues for the intellectual stimulation, but he valued even that less than he once did.

Quentin was less afraid than he had been of living at The Studio alone, especially as his whole mind set had changed and he was looking forward to expanding his social life generally, and the Studio was going to be a great place for entertaining. Nevertheless he liked the idea of Ursula sharing it with him. She was good company and they had such a lot in common and, let's face it, they were used to each other, were comfortable with each other, and needn't see that much of each other if they didn't choose to.

I'll look around," she said finally. She had been weighing up whether Quentin or her present job was more important to her, and Quentin had won. "If I can find something suitable in or around Oxford I'll come and be your lodger." The fact that she didn't particularly like the flat she owned in a dreary little London Street made the decision easier even though she could find herself taking a drop in salary, and she could always let the flat out.

Sid came back from the bar with pints for himself and Shane, orange juice for Wendy and Imogen and another glass of wine for Kathleen.

"That's your third," Imogen said to Kathleen. "I don't think you'd better have any more."

"She'll be all right, believe me," said Wendy.

It was true that Kathleen was getting a bit tipsy. "This is such a happy time," she said.

"Yes, it is," agreed Shane.

"So many weddings and christenings."

"Yes, you're right," said Imogen. "Piety's wedding today, our wedding next month, and then four christenings."

"What four christenings?" asked Shane, surprised.

"There's Byron and Piety's baby, Sid and Wendy's baby, Dainty and Amos's baby and our baby."

"Our baby? You never said you wanted our baby christened."

"Well, I do. Susan's talked me into it. You don't mind, do you?"

"Of course not. I think it's wonderful."

"Us girls have been talking. We're going to have them all christened together at Easter and have a big party."

"Thanks for telling us dads," said Sid.

Not far away Sheila and Simon were sitting at a small table with Tulip and Mikey. Mikey had his arm round Sheila's shoulders.

"Are you going to look for a job now that you've moved?" Mikey asked Simon. "I could do with another apprentice. I'll be losing Wendy for a bit after Christmas, or possibly a bit before, and Joe won't be available to help out because he's got a job of his own to go to in the week, and on Saturdays I won't be able to prise him apart from Natasha the way things are going."

Simon laughed. "I've found a job, thanks all the same."

"Oh? Doing what?"

"Set painting at the Bristol Old Vic."

"Wow. Posh."

"I don't know about that. It's rubbish money. Still, Amos said he can give me all the work I want at The Sceptre since Piety's already been out of commission for some weeks and Dainty may be, sooner than expected. It seems she's having a really bad time with morning sickness."

"I'm thinking of getting some part-time work myself," said Sheila, "but I don't see myself taking over from Wendy. Perhaps I could do a few hours at The Sceptre too."

"You could do a bit of reception work for me on a Saturday," said Mikey. "And a bit of shampooing. You don't have to have experience for that."

"We'll see," said Sheila. Mikey kissed the side of her face. Tulip gave him an old-fashioned look.

"That's enough, Mikey. We've got quite enough weddings and christenings for the next few months," and they all laughed.

Bit by bit the assembled company shifted and reassembled itself. Eventually Quentin found himself sitting with Kate, Piety, Byron, Chloe and Jack.

"Me and Byron bin talking," said Piety to Quentin. "We'd be mightily honoured if you would consent to be godfather to our firstborn child."

Quentin's face was a picture. For a moment he just stared at Piety, while the others all stared at him.

"Goodness, Piety, I'm speechless."

"That makes a change," said Chloe.

"Don't be cheeky, Chloe," said Kate.

"We would be honoured," said Byron. "A kind, educated gentleman like yourself could be such a help to our child."

"Quentin doesn't go to church," said Jack, "so he can't be a godfather."

"What's got into you children?" asked Kate.

"Leave 'em alone," said Piety, "They're all right."

"I think you'd make a wicked godfather," said Chloe. "I'd like a godfather like you."

"So would I," said Jack.

"'Wicked' doesn't mean 'wicked'," said Kate hastily, seeing Quentin's bemused expression. "It's kids' slang and it means the opposite."

"Yes," said Chloe, "it means 'brilliant'."

"Thanks for telling me," said Quentin. "In that case I think it's wicked of you two to ask me, but I'll think it over for a while, if that's okay." He was wondering what the next two decades might cost him.

"Sure is," said Byron.

"Are you coming to our Christmas show, Quentin?" asked Chloe.

"My dear child, it's only August!"

"I know. But I'm starting at the Curzon Academy next week and the auditions will be beginning straight away."

"And what part will you be playing?"

"Oh... " Chloe's face retreated into an unaccustomed humility. "Naomi and I will be lucky even to make the chorus, but you never know."

"Do come, Quentin," said Jack. "You can sit with me and Susan and buy the ice creams in the interval."

"Jack! Yes, Quentin, do come. David and I will be there, of course, and you could bring Ursula."

"If there's any possibility that Chloe will be in it I wouldn't miss it for the world," said Quentin. "Now, what's everyone having to drink?"